WITHDRAWN
FOR SALE

3 8002 01946 748

D0296908

Mr Micawber
Down Under

Mr Micawber
Down Under

David Barry

ROBERT HALE · LONDON

© David Barry 2011
First published in Great Britain 2011

ISBN 978-0-7090-9312-1

Robert Hale Limited
Clerkenwell House
Clerkenwell Green
London EC1R 0HT

www.halebooks.com

The right of David Barry to be identified as
author of this work has been asserted by him
in accordance with the Copyright, Designs
and Patents Act 1988

2 4 6 8 10 9 7 5 3 1

COVENTRY CITY LIBRARIES	
3 8002 01946 748 1	
ASKEWS & HOLT	16-Jan-2012
	£18.99
CEN	

Typeset in 11/15pt Sabon
Printed in the UK by the MPG Books Group

For Bob and Liz

'Until something turns up, I have nothing to bestow but advice. Annual income twenty pounds, annual expenditure nineteen pounds, nineteen shillings and sixpence – result happiness. Annual income twenty pounds, annual expenditure twenty pounds and sixpence – result misery.'

Mr Micawber in *David Copperfield* by Charles Dickens
1812–1870

'Mr Micawber is going to a distant country, expressly in order that he may be fully understood and appreciated for the first time. It is evident to me that Australia is the legitimate sphere of action for Mr Micawber!'

Mrs Micawber in *David Copperfield* by Charles Dickens
1812–1870

'How did it happen, how could it happen, that the man who created Micawber could pension him off at the end of the story and make him a successful colonial mayor? Micawber never did succeed, never ought to succeed; his kingdom is not of this world.'

G. K. Chesterton 1874–1936

PART ONE

1

Mrs Micawber's Clock

FOLLOWING HEAVY AUTUMN rains, the streets of Melbourne became more appropriately known as 'the swamps' by some of the long-suffering residents. Mud was everywhere. Deep holes of it pitted the main streets like moon craters; traffic became bogged down by it as wheels failed to turn and hoofs stuck fast; and pedestrians sank knee deep in its unrelenting, clammy tenacity and floundered helplessly, wading as if through treacle. Mud! Meandering aimlessly through the wide thoroughfares like a big brown river in full flood. Ubiquitous mud! It sucked and oozed and squelched and splashed, and left its dirty imprint everywhere. It showed no respect for the genteel and somehow managed to find its way into the most sterile, hygienic and God-fearing homes. Housemaids cursed the extra work it brought. Children were yelled at for forgetting to wipe their feet. Clothing became permanently encrusted with thick layers of it and the most delicate hands became coarse and rough. Immigrants, after stoically suffering and surviving the perils of the high seas, stepped ashore at Port Phillip and wept to see how quickly this unwelcome morass befouled their precious belongings. Grog-shop floors (never clean at the best of times) swam in an unholy stench of mud, dung and liquor. Nowhere was sacred. Muddy footprints everywhere – from the inner sanctum of Melbourne's finest private club to places of worship. Without exception, everyone hated with a vengeance the vile omnipresence of the brown slime and invented the most obscene euphemisms to describe it. There was not a single being of the entire population of the city of Melbourne in the autumn of 1855 whose life remained unaffected by mud.

Mr Micawber perched precariously on the edge of the pavement in Collins Street, waiting for an opportunity to cross. His clothes were still wet from the last downpour, and his legs were caked with mud, which from a distance looked like brown knee-length stockings worn on top of his black tights. He wore his top hat at a rakish angle, not from sartorial daring but because the weakest part of the brim let rainwater trickle down his back, and the raffish tilt altered the direction of the flow. But at least the rain had stopped prior to his arrival in Collins Street, and the sun was shining weakly through the sombre clouds.

Collins Street was chaotic and congested; crossing it was a risky business. Mr Micawber spent a few moments deliberating on the intricacies and timing of the Olympian sprint that was needed to avoid being trampled on by a boisterous horse or impaled upon the shaft of a cart. He remained calm and unruffled as he watched the antics of the bogged-down travellers. Somehow, amongst all this pandemonium, he seemed out of place, looking for all the world like a dignified, though down-at-heel, actor-manager; his tasselled cane held aloft in his right hand, as if he was about to hail a hansom cab. Under normal circumstances, when the mud was not persecuting the city, he would have stood out in this brash new world like some strange and rare species of bird among a flock of ragged sparrows. But the brash new world had its own problems to contend with and Mr Micawber largely went unnoticed. Until, that is, he began to cross the street.

Motivated by a powerful instinct for self preservation, he suddenly lunged off the pavement with uncharacteristic athletic agility, and dodged across Collins Street in a record-breaking ten seconds. An eventful ten seconds, in which he missed by a hair's-breadth the backward lash of a whip being used to flay two oxen

who were struggling to extricate a brewery dray from an enormous pothole where it had sunk up to its axle; he was almost
flattened by a great chestnut gelding charging towards him like a
fiery warhorse, nostrils flaring and head shaking neurotically, its
master cursing and yelling; and he very nearly met his end three
times in quick succession: beneath the wheels of a brougham, a
post-chaise and a farm-cart. But at last, heart pounding like a
hammer, he reached the safety of the other side. And just in time!
Three long blasts on a post-horn signalled the departure of the
Ballarat coach.

Stopping to get his breath back, Mr Micawber watched as
terrified pedestrians scattered and the street became miraculously
uncongested. Another bellows blast and then – magnificent sight!
– six horses thundered along the middle of the street, pulling a
massive coach seating almost thirty passengers! This was
progress indeed, and Mr Micawber attempted to doff his hat to
the coachmen. Unfortunately his right hand was encumbered by
his cane and the moment was lost. Within seconds the coach was
gone. The spectacle over, Collins Street reverted to its former state
of confusion as horsemen, muleteers and coachmen rushed to be
the first to get their animals or the wheels of their vehicles into
the grooves left by the mighty coach.

Unbuttoning his frock coat, Mr Micawber carefully took out
from under his left arm the carriage clock he had been protecting
from the elements and was satisfied to note its pristine condition;
but when he held it to his ear, his expression changed to one of
despair. Fumbling quickly through his pockets, he found the clock
key, hurriedly set his Dear Wife's clock to what he thought was
the correct time by the ever punctual Ballarat coach, thumped the
timepiece forcefully, shook it several times, then pressed it to his
ear again. His eyes glinted with relief. The clock ticked confidently and, as far as he could tell, the movement sounded healthy
enough. Pray that it would continue to tick long enough to
conclude this vital transaction.

The pawnbroker's wife slammed down a plate piled high with steaming meat and potatoes in front of her husband, glowered at him, then stormed out of the back of the shop and returned to her kitchen. Despite not speaking to her husband for close on three weeks now, she still continued to perform her wifely duties, albeit with silent anger and resentment. The pawnbroker heard the repressed venom of his wife through the noise and clatter of the pots and pans and, as he shovelled huge portions of food into his mouth, he fed his hatred by imagining his meal was poisoned and swallowed tough lumps of mutton without chewing them. But it was the atmosphere which was poisoned, and it was into this atmosphere that Mr Micawber strutted.

As he entered, a small bell tinkled merrily and incongruously in this gloomy cave of sacrificed heirlooms and riches. The pawn-broker barely glanced up from his food and continued to devour unbelievably large portions of the meal with no respite between mouthfuls. At the sight of all this food, Mr Micawber was momentarily discomposed, licked his lips and frowned and stopped in his tracks. He watched as a stream of gravy spurted from the side of the pawnbroker's mouth, and stared with wide-eyed fascination as it ran across the man's ample chin, where it got caught in a forest of dark stubble. The pawnbroker reminded Micawber of an ogre from a tale by the Brothers Grimm, and for one split-second he seriously contemplated abandoning his mission; but, as he hesitated in the oppressive silence, the ogre spoke in an expressionless voice that came from the bottom of a deep well.

'Clocks have a habit of stopping,' he boomed. His enormous Adam's-apple bobbed like a walnut in his throat as he swallowed a tricky bit of tough, gristly mutton. 'Permanently,' he added.

But having come thus far, and realizing that time was definitely not on his side, Mr Micawber persevered. He placed the clock on the counter in front of the pawnbroker's dinner plate.

'With all due respect, sir,' he began slowly, 'horologists have marvelled at its mechanical movements, giving no mere estimation of the passage of the noon sun over the meridian at Greenwich. In short, it is most reliable.'

'Get to the point!' snapped the pawnbroker, nearly losing the food from his mouth, which he just managed to catch and gulp like a ravenous dog.

Mr Micawber coughed delicately before continuing, and when he spoke it was in the measured, refined tone he reserved for simpletons.

'I was under the perceptible impression,' he enunciated, savouring each consonant, 'that the point – although circumnavigated by my testimony as to the accuracy and efficiency of this elegant contraption – had, in short, been reached.'

The pawnbroker stopped eating and looked up slyly. 'How much?' he demanded.

Mr Micawber suppressed a smile, knowing that his fish was hooked. But he still liked to retain a certain amount of propriety and dignity in transactions of this sort, for to arrive at an agreed price expeditiously seemed indelicate.

The ogre stared at Micawber, waiting for an answer.

Mr Micawber coughed more loudly. 'Ahem! Until such time as this precious ornament may be redeemed, and until such time as something turns up – which I am confidently expecting – shall we say – um – three pounds?'

The ogre began eating again. 'I'll give you one,' he mumbled, through a mouthful of potato.

Micawber reeled back with exaggerated horror. '"O death where is thy sting?"' he intoned dramatically. 'This is an heirloom, sir, handed down by my Dear Wife's progenitors. Must we be torn from our heritages and still be unable to sever pecuniary shackles? You may as well take a knife and plunge it deep into my bosom. You would be doing me a service.'

The theatricality of this speech was lost on the pawnbroker, whose attention was now closely directed towards the clock, scrutinizing its face for any progress the large hand had made since its vendor had begun to haggle.

'Er – you said one,' Micawber hastily conceded. 'Would that be a pound or a guinea?'

'Pound,' sneered the pawnbroker; and that, coupled with his unprepossessing appearance, was intimidatingly conclusive.

Micawber shrugged compliantly and tapped out a gentle rhythm with his fingers on the top of his cane, while the ox-like brute of a moneylender leaned forward on his creaking, rickety stool and brought out from under the counter eight half-crown pieces, a pawn-ticket and a tiny stub of a pencil. After licking the tip of the pencil, he scrawled something illegible across the ticket, then pushed it across the counter towards Micawber, who managed to control a relieved sigh and, with the dexterity of a conjuror, completed the transaction by surrendering the clock key and pocketing the money and pawn ticket. Then, noticing how the pawnbroker was staring fixedly at the clock's hands, he was panicked into making a token protest at the unfairness of the exchange by way of a distraction.

'It mortally aggrieves me,' he began nervously, easing away from the counter a fraction, 'that for a mere shilling you have opted to foreclose on my goodwill and custom – in short, a compromise was not reached. However, as you were the one holding the purse strings, one pound will have to suffice.'

Micawber, seeing the ogre comparing the hands on his Dear Wife's clock to those of another clock, decided it was time to hasten his departure. He turned around sharply and scuttled to the door.

'Just a minute!'

Fear froze him for an instant, his hand upon the shop doorhandle. He saw with horror that the moneylender had picked up the clock and was about to listen to its movements.

'"Time and tide await no man!"' Micawber blurted out. 'I shall therefore bid you good day, sir.'

Still clutching at faint vestiges of courtesy, Micawber brazenly but clumsily doffed his hat before exiting smartly. The shop bell tinkled again. The pawnbroker, not a man burdened by excessive intelligence, was confused and frustrated by the events which had suddenly overtaken him. How had he managed to lose control of the situation? He held the clock pressed close against his left ear. Silence. He tried the right ear. Nothing. The clock had stopped. He shook it, banged it angrily on the counter, and stared for a while at his unfinished meal, for which he seemed to have lost his appetite. And it seemed to be this, more than the clock, which sent him spinning into a convulsion of rage. As he erupted, his stool clattered to the floor.

'Maggie!' he bellowed.

The walls of the shop reverberated with hatred that was now directed towards his wife.

As for Micawber, he had already strutted briskly into the nearest wine merchant and was animatedly choosing a bottle of the very best port.

2

A Man of Few Words

MRS CAMILLA BEGS sipped her tea daintily and waited for her son to speak. She turned towards Young Emma Micawber, hoping she would say something and end the awkward silence, but both of them seemed to be stuck for words. Perhaps the strained silences were the constraints imposed on a young couple who feel they are being chaperoned. She gazed across the lawn at Melbourne, which lay below them like so many dolls' houses, and she was glad to be so far away from the mud and confusion. She felt like the monarch herself, sitting beneath the porticoes of her imposing mansion, looking down on the rest of the world.

Young Emma Micawber stifled a contented yawn. The velvety softness she felt from the warmth of the weakening sun tricked her into thinking she was blissfully happy. But deep inside her there was a struggle going on. She yearned for emotions that were more sanguine than this. She wanted to be transported. She knew she was in love, yet all she felt was a contentment and deep affection towards him. Rather like the mild and pleasurable emotion one feels when stroking a cute and helpless kitten.

The object of her affections, Ridger Begs, cleared his throat raspingly. His mother threw a frown in his direction. The silence was drawn out to breaking point.

Mrs Begs stretched a delicate hand towards the teapot. 'More tea, Emma?'

Young Emma shook her head vigorously. 'No thank you, Mrs Begs.'

'Ridger?' Mrs Begs offered her son, half-heartedly.

Irritatingly, Ridger cleared his throat again before speaking. 'No thanks, Mother.'

Mrs Begs sighed. 'I can't believe how quiet you both are. Not because of me, surely?'

Ridger looked sullen and stared into the distance beyond Melbourne. Emma glanced at him, wondering if she would always have to come to his rescue like this.

'Oh, no, Mrs Begs. Your presence is most welcome. Most welcome.'

Her words were gushing and the sentiment over elaborate, and Emma felt her cheeks burning. But Mrs Begs appeared not to notice.

'Thank you. Are you sure you won't have any more tea?'

To make up for the awkwardness she felt, Young Emma decided to be firm on this point. 'Quite sure, thank you.'

There was another hiatus. Emma looked longingly at Ridger, willing him to speak. His face was expressionless, but she could tell there was an inner struggle going on. She could tell by the trapped animal look in his green eyes. He was good-looking in a youthful way; his golden-blond hair was boyishly attractive, though his chin boasted a masculine dimple, as if it had been chiselled by a sculptor. His cheeks and jaw were smooth and downy, rather than aggressively male, and his lips were sensual and feminine. His was most definitely a handsome face, Emma decided, which might even improve with a little weathering. If only he were more gifted in the art of conversation.

She watched his lips parting, and he made a little guttural sound prior to speaking. She leaned forward eagerly in her seat. But his eyes glazed over and his mouth snapped shut like a fish. Disappointed, Emma clasped her hands together and looked down at the tablecloth. She was embarrassed, but to her suitor it seemed as if she found his procrastination irritating. Inside his head a clock was ticking and the pressure was mounting. He struggled to speak but his mind was a blank. If only he could think of something intelligent to say to break this deathly silence. But suddenly, like a spark igniting, something clicked into place inside his brain. His eyes lit up and he grinned, confident that he had been struck by divine inspiration.

'Have I ever told you about my kangaroo hunting?'

His mother gasped. 'Ridger! I'm sure Miss Micawber isn't interested in your manly exploits.' She gave Emma an apologetic smile. 'He's been full of himself ever since his little excursion towards the interior.'

Hot-flushed and squirming, Ridger gazed forlornly at Emma as if he wanted her to rescue him from this ordeal worse than death. Her heart went out to him. She smiled sympathetically and attempted to sound sincere.

'Oh, but I'd be *most* interested.'

'You would?' said Mrs Begs, with an exaggerated demonstration of amazement.

Even Ridger appeared surprised by the sincere nature of the interest shown in his escapades. He sat up and gave Emma a thankful grin. Her resolve to help him out began to dwindle.

'Well – I ...' she muttered. But seeing the light disappear from his eyes, she leaned forward and tried to sound enthusiastic. 'Tell me about the kangaroo hunt.'

Ridger didn't need to be asked twice. He was up and running. Here was a safe topic of conversation.

'Well, the problem with roo hunting is they won't keep still long enough for you to take decent aim.'

Emma's eyes widened theatrically, as if spellbound by his bravery. 'What are they like? Are they dangerous?'

Ridger laughed. 'Kangaroos? Dangerous? Of course not. They just hop about. They're like overgrown mice.'

Emma was horrified. She associated mice with her recent childhood, a time of innocence and wonder. She had been introduced to these clever and innocent creatures through her dear papa's wonderful stories. And to imagine mice, however large they were, being shot at by grown men on horseback ... well!

'Oh! Poor little things,' she squealed. 'I adore mice.'

Mrs Begs, who had been sidetracked into her own dreams and wishes, returned to the present and decided it was time to intervene.

'There!' She waved a finger at her son. 'You've succeeded in upsetting Emma. I'm going to see cook about dinner. Please see if you can find a more fitting topic of conversation to entertain a young lady while I'm gone.'

Ridger looked suitably contrite while his mother rose gracefully like a ballerina, gently shook a few crumbs from her napkin, then folded it neatly and placed it on the table. She took a last look at the landscape, as she always did, before going indoors, squinting as she surveyed the distant masts of the sailing ships at Port Phillip, a nostalgic reminder of a distant land she still regarded as home.

Emma smiled gratefully as Mrs Begs departed. She felt relieved to be left alone with Ridger. No longer constrained by his mother's presence, Emma hoped her suitor might become a model of articulation. Her hopes were dashed as she watched his face reddening and he struggled to speak. Again, she had to come to his rescue.

'It's beautifully quiet here,' she sighed. 'Peaceful.'

Ridger was still at a loss. 'Yes – I—' was all he could manage.

Emma frowned. How could this handsome young man seem so ill at ease? He looked as if a cake crumb had become lodged in his throat. She began to feel irritated. 'Is something the matter?' she asked, her voice betraying her thoughts.

'It's just ...' he began.

Emma perched on the edge of her seat hopefully; her eyebrows rose in anticipation.

Ridger gazed adoringly at her, searching her beautiful face for inspiration. How could such strange-looking parents be blessed by such loveliness? He loved to watch her when she couldn't see him; her high cheekbones and marble complexion, and the delicate nose that tilted upwards pertly, were a sight to behold. And those eyes! They were like precious blue gemstones set in pure white alabaster. And her long auburn hair, fiery and spirited, like the mane on his father's favourite stallion.

If only he could find the words to tell her how he felt.

'It's just,' he continued, 'that I've wanted to talk to you alone for ages and as soon as I get the chance....' It seemed like a long sentence and he ran out of steam. Suddenly, as if he found his ineptitude irritating, he blurted out, 'Oh hang it all! I'm not one for making speeches. Why don't we get spliced?'

Emma's expression was one of frozen stupefaction. When she recovered, her voice rose incredulously. 'Get spliced! Get spliced!'

'I realize it might seem a trifle sudden.'

'Surely this is not a proposal of marriage.'

Now that Ridger had got it off his chest, he gained some confidence.

'Well, it's not an invitation to a kangaroo hunt. So how about it? Oh, I know I should have – er – expressed myself a little better, but—'

Emma placed a hand on his, sympathetically. 'No, it is exactly what I would have expected of you, my poor sweet Ridger.'

Ridger felt a tingle running from the hand resting under hers to his loins. He smiled at her foolishly. 'Words have never been my strong point, you see.'

Emma reflected on this for a moment before speaking.

'I don't mind that. There are more than enough orators in my family.'

'Then – er – will you do me the – er – honour of accepting my hand in marriage?'

Ridger looked pleased with himself. At last he had found the right words! But Emma took her hand away from his, and stared down at her empty tea plate.

'I'm sorry, Ridger. I can't give you an answer. You know I can't.'

'Because of our parents? But suppose I had a word with my father.'

Emma stared wistfully at her left hand and tried to picture it with rings on her fingers. She sighed softly before speaking. 'I don't think it would do much good.'

'It might,' Ridger said with forced optimism. 'Especially if your father were to make a small gesture towards the arrears.'

Emma shook her head sadly. 'Poor Papa. He's had lots of bad luck. If he has found nothing remunerative today, I dread to think how he must be suffering.'

Had his daughter owned a crystal ball, and had such a tool of wizardry enabled her to look into it and see at that precise moment how affected her father was by his reduced circumstances, she would have been surprised to see him walking home jauntily along Collins Street, humming merrily, and carrying a bottle of port, a bottle of claret and a large chicken.

3

Young Emma Micawber's Piano

THE HOOFS OF Pellinore Crestfall's horse made squelching, sucking sounds as it laboured up the incline, pulling the creaking cart towards the Micawbers' house, a two-storey timber building, raised above the ground, with a veranda running along the front. The horse snorted loudly as Crestfall gently tugged the reins and stopped the horse level with the front door. The rotund tradesman turned his head sharply towards the living-room window and saw the curtain falling back into place.

'Ah hah!' he exclaimed. 'Caught you.'

With an exceedingly agile movement for such a large person, he stood and jumped from the cart, managing to avoid a deep puddle, and stamped loudly up the front steps. He rapped his knuckles so hard on the front door that he winced with pain. But he welcomed the pain as incentive in dealing with this situation. The pain helped to ignite the anger that had been fermenting on his journey. For Crestfall knew he was a soft touch and was not the bruiser he appeared. Although he gave the impression that he was capable of twelve rounds as a bare-knuckle fighter, it was entirely superficial. The wild unkempt hair which surrounded his rock-hard, moon face disguised an artistic, sensitive soul; and the scar which ran down his cheek was not from duelling or being slashed in a knife fight, but from a more mundane accident in childhood (he had fallen from his rocking horse and been wounded by a tin soldier).

He allowed his anger to simmer as he waited and listened. He thought he could hear scuffling sounds from inside the house. He knew someone was at home because he had seen the curtain drop back into place, and he fancied he had seen Micawber's face peering from behind the lace.

He knocked again, this time twice as hard, and winced again. 'Come on, Micawber! I know you're in there. I want my money. D'you hear me? I want my money.'

Pleased that he had at last risen to the challenge of confrontation, Crestfall continued hammering painfully with his knuckles. The door was suddenly flung open and he was challenged by a small, sullen, rodent-like young woman.

'Yes?'

At first, Crestfall thought he might have chosen the wrong house, and glanced around at the cluster of houses nearby. They all looked similar, but he was certain he had come to the right place because on the veranda was a rocking chair, and on top of the chair lay a copy of William Shakespeare's *The Tempest*, and Crestfall remembered the last time he had called on a similar mission, Mr Micawber had been learning speeches from this book.

Crestfall looked down at the woman with what he hoped was an intimidating expression.

'Who are you?'

She sniffed loudly. 'Agnes. I'm the 'ousekeeper.'

Crestfall felt a wave of anger lashing him, spurring him on. 'Housekeeper! Housekeeper! What about my money?'

Agnes, who had learnt to deal with far less idle threats on the streets of Whitechapel, gave him a grimace that was both sullen and provocative. 'I dunno what yer mean.'

She began to shut the door. He pushed it open again, shouting, 'The limit has been reached, Micawber. Where are you?'

He brushed past Agnes, through the small hall towards the living room.

''Ere! Where d'you fink you're going?' Agnes demanded.

Pushing open the door, and taking a deep breath ready to launch his verbal attack upon Mr Micawber, Crestfall was surprised to find three cowering figures seated on a *chaise-longue*: Mrs Micawber, with her twins, a boy and a girl, huddled either side of her like delicate china bookends. Crestfall was momentarily ruffled.

'Oh! I was looking for *Mr* Micawber.'

Mrs Micawber looked on the verge of tears and spoke as a tragedian might moments before the curtain falls.

'As you can see, Mr Crestfall, Mr Micawber – alas – is not present.'

Hovering at the door, peeved and puffing indignantly, Agnes said, 'Shall I show 'im out?'

Mrs Micawber wriggled uncomfortably. 'Shall I show the *gentleman* out? The *gentleman*, Agnes.'

Unimpressed by his status, and annoyed that an enemy had managed to slip her defences, Agnes continued to glare rudely at Crestfall.

'Now then, Mr Crestfall, to what do we owe this unexpected pleasure?'

Mrs Micawber smiled at him graciously, as if he was a welcome visitor arriving to pay his respects.

'You know very well why I'm here.'

A cloud blotted out Mrs Micawber's smile. 'Agnes, take my darlings into the nursery, would you? And give them some supper.'

'What'll I give 'em? Fresh air?'

Mrs Micawber gave Crestfall a feeble smile and an apologetic shrug, as if he must surely understand the difficulties she had with her domestics. The twins spoke in unison.

'But, Mama, we want to stay....'

Mrs Micawber clapped her hands to silence them.

'Now run along. Mama will be in to see you shortly.'

Reluctantly, the nine-year-olds abandoned their curiosity and shuffled over to Agnes, who ushered them out, but not before giving Crestfall a look of undisguised hatred and contempt, as if he was personally responsible for any harm which might befall them. She slammed the door behind her and Mrs Micawber winced. Left alone with her, Crestfall felt uncomfortable and didn't know what to do with his hands. He decided to fold them across his chest.

'You won't object if I wait for your husband?'

Mrs Micawber made an imperious gesture. 'Please make yourself comfortable.'

Crestfall unfolded his arms and eased himself into a winged armchair. But he felt as if he was losing control of the situation and softening as he had the time before. He leapt up and waved his arms about before he was able to find his voice.

'I won't be placated. Full settlement within the month, that's what I was promised.'

He walked over to an upright piano and tapped it with the flat of his hand.

'This is a fine instrument. The very latest upright. Why, the cost of the shipping alone…. If Mr Micawber is unable to make me a substantial offer, I'm afraid I shall have no alternative but to repossess.'

Mrs Micawber shuddered and gulped back her tears, and Crestfall wondered how he would cope with her in full flood. But her eyes, he noticed, remained dry.

'It is all my fault,' she sniffed. 'Mr Micawber is blameless in this matter. I thought the piano indispensable to our daughter's education. You are an artist, Mr Crestfall – surely you understand?'

'I understand about selling, Mrs Micawber, not performing. It has been many years since I gave a recital.'

'Such a waste. You have such talent.'

Crestfall opened his mouth to protest and Mrs Micawber continued hurriedly, 'I heard you play. Your demonstration.'

'Well, I try to keep my hand in.'

'Mr Liszt himself would not have been shamed.'

Having been sidetracked by the compliments, this outrageous flattery pulled him up short.

'Mrs Micawber, this time I won't be fobbed off by promises. The day of reckoning has arrived. This time I want my money.'

'And you shall have it, Mr Crestfall.'

'When?'

Incapacitated by this question, Mrs Micawber remained silent. Crestfall became heated again.

'Good heavens! You people are living beyond my means. Do you think it just and proper to employ a retinue of servants while my bill remains unpaid?'

Mrs Micawber looked genuinely puzzled. 'Retinue of servants! Whatever do you mean?'

'Well, there's your housekeeper for a start. That girl – Agnes....'

Mrs Micawber laughed. 'Housekeeper! Agnes! Agnes is nothing more than a maid, and never will aspire to anything in the domestic sense, I fear. Servants are a terrible problem here. Perhaps they find the journey unsettling.'

'I'm afraid you're missing the point—'

Mrs Micawber raised a hand to stop Crestfall from continuing. 'On the contrary: Mr Micawber and I realize we may have been somewhat lavish on occasion, but let me assure you that not one hour ago Mr Micawber spoke of meeting the pecuniary demands made of him by resorting to careful husbandry and frugality.'

Crestfall sighed deeply and sank into the winged armchair. He felt washed out, as though he had just ridden through the blackest of storms. Mrs Micawber gazed at him sympathetically.

'Please understand, Mr Crestfall, when Mr Micawber and I took on these commitments, Mr Micawber had turned his attention to stilts.'

'To what, Ma'am?'

'Stilts. Mr Micawber, being a man of talent, deduced that the answer to Melbourne's lost battle with the elements lay in stilts. It is most unfortunate that the people of Melbourne did not share the same clear view as Mr Micawber. However, I still have faith in Mr Micawber's abilities. He assures me that something will soon turn up. And please let me assure you, Mr Crestfall, that you will be the first beneficiary of his good fortune.'

Mrs Micawber felt she was now in control of the situation. Unfortunately, *Mr* Micawber, who knew of a short cut from Collins Street to the rear of their home, had entered through the back door and had therefore not spotted Crestfall's horse and cart, bounded into the living room, excitedly brandishing his recent purchases. He failed to see Crestfall in the armchair, and also missed the warning signals in his wife's eyes.

'My dear!' he said. 'I bring creature comforts and good cheer. Tomorrow we will make reductions, but today – hang the expense! Today we are prodigal.'

Like a volcano about to erupt, Crestfall rose slowly from the chair. Micawber was stilled like a sudden death, but it was for the briefest of moments. He recovered rapidly.

'Ah! My dear Pellinore.'

'Don't you "dear Pellinore" me.'

Mr Micawber glanced nervously towards the piano. 'I take it you are here about that fine instrument. But surely the Pythagorean gamut is not to be run already? In short – does it need tuning?'

'No, it does not need tuning,' Crestfall yelled. 'It needs paying for, that's what it needs.'

Mr Micawber nodded vigorously, placed his purchases on the sideboard, and then gesticulated with both arms held out towards Crestfall. 'Forgive me, my dear – er – Pelly. Because of a momentary lapse, due in part to my brief odyssey in search of pecuniary emoluments, it quite slipped my mind. But I am pleased to inform you that I am now in funds. And, while unable to expedite the obligation *in toto* – I can, in short, let you have something on account.'

Mrs Micawber clapped her hands triumphantly. 'I said Mr Micawber would turn up trumps!'

With a grandiloquent gesture, Micawber slipped his hands inside his waistcoat pocket, took out two half-crowns and offered them to Crestfall with the satisfied air of a man who is true to his word.

Crestfall stared at the coins with stunned disbelief. 'What's this?' he asked hoarsely.

'Er – I am only too aware that it is but a gesture, and settlement remains temporarily out of reach—'

Crestfall's eyes were bulbous with incredulity. 'Five shillings! I don't believe it. Do you realize how much you still owe me?'

Micawber tried to sound nonchalant. 'It is only until such time as something turns up.'

Crestfall snatched the coins and stuffed them into his pocket.

'Yes, my men, to fetch the piano, first thing tomorrow morning.'

He started for the door. Micawber leapt in front of him, barring the way, and pleaded as if he were pleading for his life.

'Just one week more. I beseech you.'

'Not another hour. Stand aside.'

'I beg of you. This is a matter of life and death.'

'It is a piano!' shouted Crestfall. 'A luxury. And one you can ill afford. How can it possibly be a matter of life and death?'

'Because,' began Micawber, thinking quickly, 'I shall kill myself.'

Mrs Micawber gasped as her precious husband bounded over to the window and attempted to raise it.

'Wilkins!' she cried. 'What are you doing?'

'Throwing myself from the window.'

Mrs Micawber screamed hysterically. 'Stop him, someone!'

Red-faced, Micawber struggled to open the window which appeared to be jammed, crying pitifully, 'Oh the disgrace! Oh the ignominy! I shall end it all.'

'Not from the ground floor you won't,' said Crestfall.

Undaunted by Crestfall's observation, Micawber lunged dramatically to the sideboard, pulled open a drawer and grabbed a knife from the cutlery canteen, intending to show Crestfall how intent on suicide he was.

'Then blood must be spilt,' he intoned. 'It is a noble way to die. *Et tu, Brute*! We who are about to die....'

His eyes widened in horror when he saw that he had mistakenly grabbed a dessert spoon. He quickly exchanged it for a knife. Admittedly it was only a fish knife, but at least it was a knife this time. He pressed the blade against his stomach, like a centurion about to fall on his sword.

Mrs Micawber stood and screamed. 'Wilkins! My Love! Think of your children.'

Overcome by the thoughts of her Dear Husband's bloodied corpse twitching on the living-room rug, she fainted conveniently back on to the *chaise-longue*. Micawber, glad he no longer had to impale himself upon a fish knife, leapt to her rescue.

'Emma! Dearest! Speak to me.'

As he rushed over to her, Micawber waved a hand towards the sideboard and took command. 'The smelling salts. Quickly!' he told Crestfall. Then he knelt down and attended to his wife.

'Oh, Emma, my dear. What have I done to you? Forgive me.'

Caught up in the mayhem, Crestfall tugged open one of the sideboard drawers. It contained a needlework basket.

'Second drawer down,' Micawber instructed without taking his eyes off Mrs Micawber. Crestfall handed him the bottle and he waved it under his wife's nose.

Mrs Micawber's head moved sharply away from the pungent

aroma, and she coughed. 'Is that you, Papa?' she said in a spectral voice. 'Is that you, My Dear Mama?'

'It is I,' said Micawber to his beloved. 'Your Dearest Husband.' Out of the corner of his eye, Micawber thought he detected scepticism in Crestfall's expression, and added for his benefit, 'I fear the shock has sent her reeling back in time.'

The door flew open and Agnes burst in.

'What's goin' on? I 'eard this terrible racket.'

Her eyes widened in alarm when she saw her mistress lying supine upon the *chaise-longue*.

'You all right, ma'am?'

Micawber gave a heavy, grief-laden shake of his head. 'She has received a mortal blow to the system.'

Agnes gave Crestfall a look which suggested that the dark forces of evil would one day avenge the Micawber family for this intrusion. If anything had succeeded in destroying Crestfall's resolve, it was Agnes's malevolent expression.

'I only called to collect an unpaid bill.'

Agnes's stare was unnerving and Crestfall found himself relenting.

'Very well, Micawber, you have till the end of the week....'

Mrs Micawber groaned.

'The end of *next* week.'

Crestfall made a speedy exit, glad to be out of this bedlam, but at the same time wondering how he had yet again failed in his mission. As soon as the front door slammed, signalling his departure, Mrs Micawber sat up.

'Has he gone?'

Micawber picked up the bottle of port. 'Yes, My Dearest. I think you may be in need of a tonic. And I think I may accompany you in a glass or two.'

'Huh!' exclaimed Agnes. 'All that shoutin' and carryin' on. The twins was scared to come out of the nursery, they was.'

'Poor little darlings,' said Mrs Micawber, straightening her dress. 'Tell them it was one of their Papa's dramatic recitations.'

As Agnes returned to the nursery, Micawber poured out two glasses of port, happily humming a hornpipe, as if nothing had happened.

4

Father and Son

'HERE'S TO YOUR friendship, Godfrey,' bellowed Young Wilkins above the noise and babble of the bar. He clinked his tankard rather boisterously against his new-found friend's, causing much of their dark ale to spill on to the filthy floor.

'Careful,' Godfrey admonished. 'You'll have us thrown out for dirtying the premises.'

Young Wilkins gave Godfrey a questioning look, wondering if irony was intended by his friend's remark; but Godfrey's expression was blank. Young Wilkins glanced around at the insalubrious atmosphere of the bar, before staring down at the unhygienic floor. When he looked up, Godfrey was laughing, and slapped him affectionately on the shoulder. Young Wilkins grinned and shook his head.

'For a moment I thought you were serious.'

Encouraged by his friend's sense of mischief, and by feelings of warmth and humanity after imbibing a good many tankards of ale, Young Wilkins smiled. Something took deep root inside his stomach and began to surge and grow until it was about to burst forth like a spring flower.

'I think,' he said, 'that everyone in this ale-house seems a trifle gloomy. So what do you say I entertain them with one of my comic songs?'

Godfrey, who had already witnessed one such performance, hesitated. 'Er – I don't wish to dampen your high spirits, Wilkins, but really' – he waved a disparaging hand at the murky bar – 'it may be the time, but I hardly think it's the place.'

A dark cloud eclipsed Young Wilkins's feeling of bonhomie.

'Oh,' he said flatly.

Godfrey stared at Young Wilkins. Although he hadn't known him very long, not even for twenty-four hours, he could read his new friend's feelings from his expressive face, which seemed to be made of India rubber. It was an innocent, vulnerable face and every thought and feeling showed in the malleability of his aspect.

Godfrey toasted him with his tankard and gave him a toothy grin.

'You excelled yourself in the performance you gave in the tavern last night.'

'Hmm,' Young Wilkins exclaimed doubtfully. 'At the time I thought you were very sparing in your praise.'

'Nonsense. I didn't want you to get a swollen head, that's all.'

A sudden muffled roar came from somewhere behind a door at the far end of the bar. Young Wilkins peered through the smoke, which reminded him of his childhood days in the London fog, and frowned. Glad of the distraction, Godfrey swept the hair out of his eyes before giving his friend his most charming and knowing smile.

'I expect you're wondering about that shouting.'

'It had crossed my mind.'

'Er …' Godfrey hesitated, and then his smile broadened. 'Are you in funds?'

Young Wilkins tapped his pocket with some reluctance. 'Well, I have enough for more of the same, if that's what you mean.'

'That's not what I mean. Come on, I'll show you.'

A dark infestation of dubious humanity stood between Godfrey and his objective. He hesitated briefly before taking his life in his hands and obsequiously excused his way through the fearsome crowd. Young Wilkins stuck close behind. Brushing close to a portly, inebriated man swaying from side to side, he jogged the man's elbow, causing him to spill half his beer. Young Wilkins froze for an instant and was about to apologize profusely, but the man stared down at the floor, trying to work out where his beer had gone. Wilkins hurried on and mercifully arrived at the door unscathed. Godfrey gave him a devil-may-care grin, as if he had just negotiated a far more treacherous journey than merely crossing a crowded bar, then opened the door and ushered him inside.

The room was dark and small, the ceiling low, and the stench of human sweat oppressive. In the centre of the room a crowd of men stood hunched over a long table. They were quiet now, tense and expectant, like a snake about to strike. Then suddenly a beefy roar went up. Godfrey pulled the reluctant Young Wilkins closer to the table and they both peered over the backs of the men. What they observed lasted hardly any time at all.

Two mice raced along a narrow, wooden channel, obviously purpose-built for the sport. Having been released at the same time from a trap at the starting end of the course, the mice raced towards the finishing line, on which lay a small lump of cheese. As soon as one of the mice reached the glittering prize ahead of its competitor, another great roar went up from around that table. Money changed hands, losers cursed and blasphemed, and winners had doubts cast upon their parentage.

Godfrey turned towards Young Wilkins and raised his eyebrows expectantly. His friend knew what was expected of him and began to look concerned.

'Look here, Godfrey, I really can't afford ...'

Godfrey raised a hand and smiled disarmingly. 'Oh, risk it, Wilkins. It isn't as if you've got much to lose. And, who knows, you might leave here with much more than when we arrived.'

Young Wilkins found it difficult to counter the logic of this argument. There was no getting away from it, he was tempted. He heard someone shouting:

'Place your bets on the next race. And choose your rodent!'

He took the money out of his pocket and was rewarded by one of Godfrey's broader grins.

Mr Micawber savoured his port with lip-smacking relish. Mrs Micawber stared at hers a trifle wistfully.

'My Love,' said Micawber, noticing the distant look in his Dear Wife's eyes. 'You appear to be neglecting this fine libation, which is an unspeakable pleasure.'

Mrs Micawber shook her head solemnly and said, 'My poor dear mama!'

Mr Micawber frowned deeply and looked towards the door. He was puzzled. Pellinore Crestfall must have departed at least a quarter of an hour ago and yet his Dearest appeared to be still blighted by that unfortunate scene.

'My poor dear mama!' Mrs Micawber reiterated more vehemently.

Micawber felt slightly irritated by this outburst. 'Heaven preserve us! Are you still afflicted following the assault upon our domicile?'

'I am reflecting upon a loss.' Mrs Micawber held up the port glass and examined its contents before continuing, 'This fine libation, as you put it, has cost me dearly. Another family heirloom has been squandered. A treasure is lost forever.'

'But what use is a clock that cannot inform us how the enemy progresses?'

'It could have been repaired, Wilkins.'

Micawber showed his exasperation by pointing an index finger at the floor and waving it like a pendulum. 'But no self-respecting timepiece could be expected to survive such climatological vicissitudes – winter when it should be summer, and vice versa. In short, that clock was worthless.'

'But not to *me*, it wasn't,' Mrs Micawber said, with more force than her husband thought necessary. 'It belonged to my dear mama. And we have sold so much that belonged to her. There is so little left.'

She looked down into her drink and sniffed. Mr Micawber put his drink down, went over to her and gently placed a hand upon her shoulder.

'I am sorry, My Love. I am doing my best. Something is bound to turn up.'

Mrs Micawber placed a hand on his, and they both remained still, as if posing for a portrait painter. This domestic tableau ended when Mrs Micawber looked up at her husband reproachfully.

'Bound to turn up,' he emphasized.

'I will never desert you, Wilkins, you know that. But if you don't mind my saying so, perhaps you ought to do more to assist things in turning up.'

Micawber squeezed her shoulder affectionately. 'My Angel, as usual I defer to your good sense.' He consulted his pocket watch. 'And now I think it is time for me to entertain the twins with the next instalment of *The Demon of the Moor*.'

He took a quick slurp of his drink on the way out. After he had gone, Mrs Micawber thoughtfully sipped her port. Her thoughts meandered reflectively through the English countryside. As she took another sip of her warming drink, she saw herself standing on clifftops, high above a seaside town; Hastings perhaps, or Eastbourne or Bournemouth. Her memory jumbled them up and all seaside towns merged into one idyllic setting. It was nothing short of paradise on earth. She saw herself gazing out over a calm sea with gently bobbing boats, and children scampering in and out of rock pools on a perfect sandy beach. But the perfect panorama vanished as she tilted her glass. The flood had become a trickle.

Sighing, she rose and replenished her port wine.

*

Thomas Begs breathed in noisily through his nostrils, savouring the fresh damp air as he waited by the stable door. Presently he heard the gentle clip-clop on cobbles as the enormous chestnut gelding ambled back after being put through its paces. Begs loved the sound like no other; except perhaps the flat-out pounding of hoofs on turf. As the horse rounded the corner and entered the stable yard, there was a quivering in his stomach, a sweet antici-pation, and it was moments such as these when it felt good to be alive. The jockey had dismounted and was grinning cockily as he walked the horse towards Begs.

'Well done, Declan,' Begs said. 'Looks like his fastest yet.'

He patted the horse on the neck, and the gelding raised its head and lowered it quickly as if acknowledging the compliment.

The jockey's expression became sincere and earnest, like a schoolboy trying to please a favourite teacher. 'He's never been more ready. He could outrun a Dublin pickpocket. And he's consistent.'

'Think he can beat Shelbourne's nag?'

The jockey stared curiously at his boss and noticed the traces of a secret smile on his thin lips.

'Anyone'd think you and Captain Shelbourne were mortal enemies.'

For an instant, Begs's eyes became distant. And when he spoke, his voice was distant. 'We've an old score to settle.'

The jockey realized this was as much as Begs was likely to reveal. He was a secretive man. Introspective. Except when it came to his passion. Horses.

'Well,' the jockey shrugged, 'it's a civilized way to do battle.'

He led the horse away to one of the stables, leaving Begs to his own mysterious thoughts. Ridger suddenly came tearing round the corner of the long row of stables, almost slipped in some mud, and then dashed breathlessly towards his father.

'Father,' he began hurriedly, 'I'd like a word with you—'

His father accepted his son's presence like the continuation of a previous conversation. 'I think, Ridger,' he said, 'I'm about to take some of the glory from Captain Shelbourne at last.'

Ridger, who was in no mood to listen to his father's obsession again, injected an urgent, pleading tone into his mission.

'This is important, Father—'

Either Begs was genuinely lost in his own world or deliberately chose to ignore his son. Whatever the reasons, he continued to speak about his passions, but unemotionally, as if he was deliberately holding them in check, in order to avoid some future disappointment.

'It could be the turning point for which I've waited all these years. One day soon, Melbourne will have a meeting to compare with the Royal Day at Ascot and my stables will be the best, Ridger.'

Begs turned and looked at his son, adding intensely, 'The best in this God-forsaken continent!'

'Father! You're not listening to me. I've asked Emma Micawber if she'll be my wife.'

'And?'

'And she's turned me down.'

Ridger looked utterly dejected. He craved paternal love and understanding, needed the one word from his father or the reassuring arm around his shoulder that would make everything right. Instead, his father looked openly relieved.

'Well then, that appears to be that.'

Begs sniffed, almost derisively, turned and walked away to inspect his stables and horses. Ridger dashed after him and barred his way.

'But you don't understand. I–I'm in love with Emma.'

'And is this love not reciprocated?'

'Yes. Well – no. It can't be. Not while you continue to persecute her father.'

Begs tried to control himself but there was an angry tremor in his voice. 'Now listen to me, Ridger – Micawber is just another tenant of mine, and a poor one at that. What makes you think I ought to provide him with free accommodation?'

'Nothing. I'm not saying that.'

'Well, what *are* you saying?'

'Micawber needs a bit more time, that's all.'

Begs avoided his son's eyes as he spoke. 'I regret to say it is out of my hands. You know I leave the management of my properties in the hands of Mr Larkfield.'

'How convenient for you,' Ridger snapped.

Begs chose to ignore the sarcasm and spoke in an even, measured tone. 'Mr Larkfield is a reasonable man and, knowing of your attachment to Micawber's daughter, he has been extremely lenient so far. But even he cannot allow this state of affairs to continue. Unless Micawber can pay a substantial proportion of his arrears, he will be given the order to vacate the property.'

Ridger felt the blood rush to his face. 'My God! I see now what you're up to. It's because you don't want me to marry her, isn't it?'

'No, that is not the reason.'

'Well then – why?'

Begs stared blankly at his son, unable to provide him with a satisfactory answer. The silence between them stretched to breaking point. Begs dug in his heels and refused to speak, staring deep into his son's eyes without wavering. It was Ridger who was the first to break.

'Very well. I have some money of my own. Not much, but it should be enough.'

He turned and walked away without looking back.

'Ridger!' shouted Begs. 'I forbid you to bail out Micawber. Defy me in this and you'll never marry Miss Micawber. That I can promise you.'

5

A Visit from Mr Larkfield

THE TWINS, EMILY and Edward, sat up in bed, their blankets gathered closely about them for protection, faces peering over the top, their eyes wide with fear, as their father intoned in a voice wrenched from the dark corners of his mind.

'And never was there heard such a fearful, blood-curdling howling. It was the black dog of death, come to claim another victim for the Demon of the Moor. Just as the clock began to strike the midnight hour, there came a dreaded knock upon the cottage door....'

At this instant, the cue was answered synchronously by Mr Larkfield, who thumped loudly with his cudgel upon the Micawber front door. He was, of course, unaware of the terror he had struck into the hearts of the twins, who squealed with fright and disappeared under the blankets.

'It's the black dog! The black dog!'

A shuddering exclamation issued forth from Micawber, his eyes rolled heavenwards dramatically, and he dared to point an accusatory, though imaginary, finger at the Almighty for unjustly abandoning him.

'Would that it was the phantom hound. Alas! That knock, to which I am previously acquainted, is – I fear – a more prosaic disturber of our domestic bliss. In short, it sounds like Mr Larkfield.'

Micawber patted the twins' outlines comfortingly before rising from the edge of the bed. They whispered and nudged each other and daringly peeped out from under the bedclothes.

'Fear not, My Angels,' their father reassured them. 'Your mama will visit you shortly and lullaby you gently into slumber.'

The twins waited for their father to close the door behind him before starting a pillow fight.

As Micawber came into the hall, Agnes opened the front door to Mr Larkfield, who had his cudgel raised to strike again. He also carried a black bag like a surgeon's.

''E ain't at home,' Agnes snapped.

She was about to slam the door shut in Larkfield's face, but was disconcerted to find he was paying her no attention whatsoever. In fact – the cheek of the man! – he was smiling and staring over her right shoulder.

'Who's that then?' he said. 'Shakespeare's ghost?'

Agnes, bristling at his impertinence, turned to see Micawber, arms outstretched, welcoming him like a long-lost friend.

'Ah, my dear Larkfield! Step inside. Step inside.'

Agnes glared at her master. 'Wish you'd make up your mind when you're in and when you're not in.' She stormed off to her kitchen, where she would relive the scene with Mr Larkfield and definitely hold all the trump cards.

Micawber laughed foolishly and told Larkfield, 'I should take what Agnes says *cum grano salis.*'

Larkfield seemed confused.

'With a pinch of salt,' Micawber explained.

Trying to look as if the Latin phrase had escaped him but temporarily, Larkfield muttered, 'Pinch of salt. Yes, of course.'

Micawber closed the front door and ushered Larkfield towards the parlour. He paused with his hand upon the doorknob and whispered conspiratorially to the rent collector, 'Mrs Micawber has been insalubrious of late. I fear for her health. The slightest shock may prove fatal. I trust you are not a bearer of bad tidings.'

Larkfield began to stammer awkwardly that there was just the small matter of the rent arrears, but Micawber ignored him and swung open the parlour door to reveal his wife, demurely darning one of his stockings.

'My Dearest, look who is here. Please try not to speak. I am sure Mr Larkfield will understand.' Micawber patted Larkfield on the shoulder, treating him like a sympathetic and understanding visitor. 'She is very weak at the moment.'

Falling in with her husband's approach, Mrs Micawber stared beseechingly into Larkfield's small, sunken eyes. He had a large, round face, pitted like mouldy cheese, with an unkempt sprout of jet-black hair on top of his balding head. It was neither a frightening face nor a comforting one. But Mrs Micawber was aware that the rent collector while not exactly a practitioner of philanthropy, was at least tinged by traces of humanity. She spoke to him in a faint voice.

'Mr Larkfield, how kind of you to visit. I have been making feeble attempts at some domestic repairs, but …'

As though abandoning her task through sheer effort, she let the darning drop onto her lap.

'Please don't trouble yourself, My Dear,' her husband offered, oozing kindliness. 'I am sure Agnes will complete the chores.'

Larkfield stared pointedly at her port glass.

'Medicinal,' Micawber explained hastily. 'Won't you make yourself comfortable, Mr Larkfield?'

Larkfield remained standing. 'I shall get straight to the point, Mr Micawber—'

Micawber raised a hand in supplication. 'Quite so. You are here on business. I am proud to admit that I am of a similar disposition when involved in pecuniary matters. Procrastination is the thief of time. Collar him!'

'My sentiments exactly, Mr Micawber. Now then, about the rent arrears: I am instructed by my employer …'

At this juncture Micawber glanced uneasily towards his wife, who immediately knew what was expected of her. She attempted to rise unsteadily, failed miserably, and then fell back onto her *chaise-longue*, crying, 'Oh what's to become of us? What's to become of us?'

'Emma, My Dear! Don't desert us. We need you. Think of the children.'

'Oh what's to become of us?' repeated Mrs Micawber, stretching a feeble hand towards some ghostly apparition that seemed to be beckoning from beyond the grave.

'Mark well her words,' Micawber whispered to Larkfield. 'They may well be *in extremis.*'

'I was never much of a Latin scholar.'

By way of explanation, Mrs Micawber was about to demonstrate the meaning of her husband's words when Agnes popped her head round the door.

'Shall I put the chicken on to cook, ma'am?'

Trying not to catch Larkfield's eye, Mrs Micawber nodded bravely. 'Thank you, Agnes, though it is very doubtful that any comestibles will pass these lips.'

Agnes shrugged. 'Please yourself. And the twins would like you to say goodnight.'

After the briefest pause, Mrs Micawber suddenly leapt to her feet, crying, 'No! I will rally through. I must; for the sake of the family.'

Agnes, who still hadn't forgiven the master of the house for his contrariness, muttered something unintelligible and swept out.

Micawber put an arm around his wife's shoulders. 'That's the spirit, My Love! Though I'm sure there is none who would lay blame on your burdened shoulders if your strength deserted you.' He stared at Larkfield. 'After such demolishing news.'

'I am merely the tool, Mr Micawber. The instrument. Just carrying out my duties.'

'Alas!' said Micawber mournfully, dragging himself wearily towards his scruffy but comfortable old armchair. 'It is bag and baggage into the murky streets.'

He sank into the chair like a bedraggled heap. The springs protested beneath his weight. Larkfield rummaged in his black bag and produced an eviction notice.

'I'm sorry, Mr Micawber, I truly am. If it's any consolation, you was always my favourite tenant, in spite of being a difficult payer.'

Micawber took the notice and gave it a cursory inspection. 'But the tariff is extravagant, My Dear Larkfield. Eight pounds per month to keep my family secure from the elements—'

Attempting to control his irritation, Mr Larkfield interrupted. 'The rent is cheaper than you'll find for most residences in Melbourne. Good Lord, Mr Micawber! A property such as this usually fetches a hundred and twenty pounds per annum.' He saw Micawber was about to protest and continued hurriedly, 'Ever since gold was discovered, Melbourne has become a prosperous city and the rent you are being charged is far more reasonable than any you'll find in this neighbourhood.'

Micawber placed the flat of his hand over his heart, and waved the eviction notice in front of Larkfield with his other. 'I find this hard to comprehend – the man responsible for this is our daughter's prospective father-in-law.'

'But surely you do not expect him to support you and your family simply because his son is courting your daughter?'

Aware that Larkfield's argument was unarguably logical, and also undeniably rhetorical, Mrs Micawber still felt it needed answering in no uncertain terms.

'Mr Micawber intends to honour his pecuniary commitments, Mr Larkfield, if only the commitments were not so immediately pressing.'

'In short,' Micawber added, 'I need more time.'

Larkfield gestured apologetically. 'The sands have run, Mr Micawber. You're an educated gentleman. It's always been a pleasure to converse with you. I deeply regret—'

Larkfield broke off and rummaged inside his bag. There was a clink of coins, and for one moment Micawber thought he was about to be the beneficiary of a charitable gesture. Instead, the rent collector took a book out of the bag, which Micawber recognized as *Quentin Durward*.

'Thank you for introducing me to these great works of literature. I only wish I might have had more time to finish this one.'

Larkfield surrendered the book to Micawber with some reluctance, and it crossed Micawber's mind that the rent collector, far from being sympathetic to the family's predicament, had his own selfish reasons for not wanting to see them evicted. Then Micawber looked up and, seeing the misty look in Larkfield's eyes, immediately felt guilty for thinking such censorious thoughts. He leapt up from his seat and thrust the book into Larkfield's hands.

'Oh, but you must,' he cried.

Larkfield seemed embarrassed. 'Well, in the circumstances, I don't think—'

'Nonsense, I won't hear of it. I bear no personal grudges.'

Larkfield stared uncomprehendingly at Micawber for a moment. He was unaccustomed to such acts of kindness. And, in spite of everything, Micawber actually gave him a kindly smile. Recovering from the shock of this extravagant gesture by a tenant he was about to evict, Larkfield told Mrs Micawber, 'I think you married a saint there, ma'am, if you don't mind my saying. What a shame he couldn't keep up with the rent.'

There was a scuffling noise from outside, the door was suddenly flung open, and in bounded Young Wilkins, accompanied by Godfrey. Young Wilkins was brandishing a bottle of claret.

'"Fill ev'ry glass",' he recited merrily. '"For wine inspires us, and fires us with courage, love and joy".' Then he clapped Godfrey on the back and added, 'I should like you to meet my very good and new-found friend – Godfrey McNeil.'

Mr Micawber exchanged a look of embarrassment with his

wife, wondering what impression this had made upon Larkfield, whose otherwise open countenance was now an inscrutable mask.

'Master Wilkins Micawber!' Mrs Micawber said admonishingly. 'I hope you have not been in bibulous company.'

'And making free in a fiscal way,' his father added.

Larkfield coughed loudly to signal his presence. All heads turned to look at him.

'Yes,' he said disapprovingly, 'I see Master Micawber is quite a chip of the old block.'

Mr Micawber, who still had the eviction notice in his hand, gave it to Young Wilkins.

'Perhaps this will bring you to your senses.'

Young Wilkins read it slowly. A silence fell on the room. Micawber thought he could hear the ticking of a clock and looked towards the sideboard where his dear departed mother-in-law's clock had once stood. But he was mistaken. The ticking was fanciful. And the empty space the clock had occupied was a significant reminder of his shortcomings as a provider.

Young Wilkins finished reading the notice, handed it to Larkfield and enquired, 'Is this ... irrevocable?'

Larkfield thought about it, and then replied, 'Half the arrears would stay the execution of it, so to speak.'

Like one who practises sleight of hand, Young Wilkins called out, 'Hey presto!' and, with a flourish, suddenly held up four pound notes. 'I think four pounds should just about cover it.'

Larkfield was staggered. 'Four pounds!'

'Yes,' agreed Young Wilkins, enjoying himself. 'Four is half of eight, if I'm not mistaken.'

Larkfield scowled at the money, wondering if his employer would be angered by his rash agreement to accept only half the arrears, since there was also another eight pounds due for the current month. But, infected by the delight of the assembled company, he swept the doubts from his mind and tore the eviction notice in half. His action elicited a small ripple of applause, which he acknowledged with a small bow, like an entertainer completing his performance.

'Thank you,' he said, smiling; then turned to Micawber and addressed him in a more serious tone. 'Before I am forced to return, I sincerely hope—'

Micawber interrupted him. 'That I will have secured a position with pecuniary benefits. Quite.'

'I was going to say,' continued Larkin, 'that I hope I will have finished that book at last. Good evening to you, Mr Micawber.' He acknowledged Mrs Micawber with a gracious nod. 'Ma'am.'

Larkfield dropped the book into his black bag and exited. As soon as Micawber heard the front door bang shut, he chuckled and slapped his son heartily on the back.

'Saved at the eleventh hour! But where did all that money come from?'

'We have Godfrey to thank for that,' Young Wilkins replied.

Mr and Mrs Micawber turned their attention towards their son's new friend and smiled tentatively.

'I'm sorry,' Godfrey said. 'I seem to have called at a rather inopportune moment.'

Micawber shook him warmly by the hand. 'Not at all. Not at all. You are most welcome. Most welcome.'

Mrs Micawber clapped her hands in delight. 'It seems we have found a benefactor.'

Godfrey's smile widened. 'Oh, I've done little really. I merely provided Wilkins with an opportunity; pointed him in the right direction, as it were. It was he who provided the capital.'

The Micawbers stared at their son, waiting for him to elaborate.

'But how was it,' his father asked, 'that you managed to raise such a substantial sum?'

Young Wilkins frowned. He realized he was in a jam, having to provide his father with a satisfactory explanation of how he came by his good fortune.

6

Sensible and Impetuous

WHILE RIDGER WAS talking to his father at the stables, Emma Micawber waited for the carriage that was to take her home. Mrs Begs, who liked this sensible girl, and was under no illusions about her son's social inadequacies, thought Miss Micawber would be a perfect match and might give Ridger the confidence he needed. And so, while they waited for the carriage to be brought round, Mrs Begs questioned and probed, politely delving into Emma's character, searching for the deep flaw that someone with parents such as hers would be bound to inherit; but, apart from a rather capricious fondness for the arts and, with her love of books, a tendency to often escape into the world of fiction. Mrs Begs could find almost no imperfections in her character. Her parents, on the other hand, were the greatest stumbling block to what in all other respects seemed like the perfect union.

As Emma Micawber climbed aboard the carriage, Mrs Begs watched from the balcony above the crescent-shaped drive, holding back the tears of disappointment that threatened her calm, almost regal, demeanour. It was such a shame! She knew her husband would never accept a daughter-in-law with such a wastrel for a father. If only Micawber could attain some financial stability, however modest, then she was certain wedding bells would not be out of the question. But, from what she had learnt of Mr Micawber, this seemed unlikely, and her heart dropped like a stone into a well of gloom.

As Emma Micawber sat back in the carriage, she waved and smiled her farewell. But so saddened was Mrs Begs by thoughts that she was losing a fine daughter-in-law, she was incapable of returning the smile. The carriage pulled away and Mrs Begs allowed her tears to flow freely now that she was unobserved.

She felt as if she was playing a role in a melodrama, and Miss Micawber was not merely departing following a pleasant after-noon tea, but was leaving forever, never to be seen again. It was partly indulgence, allowing her emotions to escape; but it was also a genuine disappointment, masking the true dream of a woman who so wanted a daughter, and had only been once blessed with a son.

She stood rigid on the balcony, like an alabaster statue, and dabbed at her tears with a tiny lace handkerchief. Ten minutes went by, and still she remained rooted to the spot, tormented by her shame and hypocrisy.

'Mother!'

Mrs Begs hadn't heard her son approaching and was startled. She wheeled around to face him, hoping her eyes were not red from crying; but Ridger seemed agitated and appeared to be inwardly fighting some conflicting emotions.

'Has Emma gone home?' he asked, glancing towards the drive.

'Yes, of course. You know she has. You were the one who asked Jimmy to bring the carriage around.'

Ridger smacked his leg impatiently with an open palm. 'How long? How long has she been gone?'

Mrs Begs frowned. 'Ten, perhaps fifteen minutes. Why?'

Ridger's agitation grew, and his mother watched as he made a sudden move, then stopped as if he was undecided about some-thing. She saw the inner conflict in her son resolved as he nodded to himself and smacked a fist into his palm.

'Right!' he snapped. 'I should catch her before she gets home.' He strode across the balcony towards the steps.

Alarmed, Mrs Begs called after him. 'Ridger! What are you

going to do? Please don't do anything to upset your father.' As he raced down the flight of steps, she heard him mutter, 'To hell with my father.'

As the carriage shuddered and creaked through the muddy streets, Emma Micawber sat gripping the edge of her seat, while the driver coaxed the horse with unintelligible exclamations.

Tense and confused since leaving the Begs house, Emma wore a permanent frown. She wondered about Mrs Begs, who had seemed superficially friendly, but somehow guarded and secretive, as if she had something to hide; and when Emma had politely asked her about her life in England, she had changed the subject. The past appeared to be a forbidden topic of conversation.

Lost in troubled thoughts, Emma hadn't noticed the commotion that was going on around her; the angry cry of the coachman, the shuddering of the carriage and exclamations of surprise. As she raised her head, squinting from the setting sun that was a halo around the horseman who had suddenly appeared beside the carriage, she heard Ridger's voice crying, 'Whoa!'

Ridger grabbed and pulled at the halter of the horse pulling the carriage.

'Careful, sir!' cautioned the driver. 'You could have a nasty fall. You only had to ask me to stop and I'd have done so.'

The coachman's pragmatism was lost on Ridger who had seized the opportunity to show off in a rather swashbuckling manner. The carriage ground to a halt with a squelch of mud, sounding unromantically mucky.

'Ridger!' cried Emma. 'What are you doing? Be careful.'

The coachman, adopting an apologetic, subservient tone, took advantage of the young upstart's impetuousness to admonish him.

'I'm sorry, sir, I have orders to drive Miss Micawber directly to her home.'

Ridger waved it aside. 'This won't take a minute, Jimmy.' He handed Emma a leather purse. 'Please give this to your father, with my compliments.'

Emma reached out, and then quickly drew back her hand, as if the purse might burn her. 'What are you giving me?'

Ridger's horse turned away suddenly, and he tugged on the rein with his free hand, pulling it full circle so that he was facing Emma again. 'I'm giving you some money. Not much. Five pounds. It's all that I have. But it should be enough to keep Mr Larkfield from—'

'Ridger!' Emma broke in. 'Does your father know about this?'

Ridger shook the purse defiantly in front of her. 'It's my money. It's got nothing to do with him.'

'I cannot accept it. Ridger, my sweet! I know why you're doing it, but you're being impetuous and foolish. It's not the way to solve this problem.' She leant forward in her seat and spoke to the driver. 'Will you take me home, please? Immediately.'

'Yes, miss.'

The driver cracked the horse's reins sharply and the carriage jolted and shot forward, leaving Ridger staring after it looking confused and hurt. He couldn't understand Emma's reasons for turning down his offer to help, and he wondered why life had to be so complicated.

He watched the carriage as it rattled away from him. When it had gone a little distance, Emma turned back, gave him a small wave and a pitying smile. But it was no consolation, and he felt a surge of anger which was directed towards his father, the person he most blamed in this affair.

Brutally wheeling his horse around, he set off for home.

7

Optimism Returns

M R MICAWBER, YOUNG Wilkins and Godfrey were in high spirits as they stood waiting to be seated at the dining table, and watched as Agnes placed a roasted chicken in the centre. Micawber sighed contentedly and smiled at Godfrey, studying him carefully for the first time. Although not handsome, the young man's face was pleasantly rounded, with a squat nose, and he had auburn curly hair and chocolate-coloured eyes. He was the man in the street, a face you would have to see many times to remember it.

But Micawber was immediately taken by him and clapped him on the shoulder.

'Any friend of my son has a personal claim upon my services and you are cordially invited to share in our repast.'

Godfrey, who had already been invited to stay for dinner, thanked Micawber once more, while Agnes moved dishes containing vegetables to new positions about the table. She stood back and surveyed her work with a critical eye as Mrs Micawber entered.

'Thank you, Agnes,' Mrs Micawber said. 'They are both sound asleep.'

'Ma'am,' Agnes replied dutifully, though she frowned uncertainly, wondering if she was expected to stay and dish out the vegetables. She hovered indecisively. Mrs Micawber fixed her with a steady look.

'Mr Micawber will carve. I think we can manage.'

Realizing she would no longer be privy to the private conversation of her employers and their guest, Agnes swept out ill-temperedly and slammed the door. Mrs Micawber smiled at the assembled company, giving no indication that she had noticed her servant's petulant display, and sat at one end of the short refectory-style table.

Micawber moved to the other end of the table, gestured expansively for his son and Godfrey to be seated, and they sat opposite one another. Now that his gastric juices were aroused, Godfrey leant forward and spoke with unbridled enthusiasm.

'I can still hardly believe how that little fellow romped home, just when it was all or nothing.'

Micawber coughed loudly for attention. 'Before we regale ourselves, I feel it is my bounden duty to cast a little gloom over the proceedings.' He fixed his gaze on Young Wilkins. 'While it is fortuitous that this promiscuous venture of yours has delivered us from our present misfortunes, it is your filial duty, young sir, to heed my warning. Put not your trust in fate, in the spin of a coin or the throw of a dice. Chance has been generous to you on this occasion, because you are a novitiate at her game. The lady is kind to virgin speculators. In short ...'

He paused before rewarding them with his précis. Unfortunately, Godfrey leapt in with the summing-up.

'It was beginner's luck!'

Micawber's composure was momentarily thrown and he struggled to continue. He spoke to Godfrey exceedingly slowly and pointedly. 'It was indeed beginner's luck, as I was about to conclude.'

Mrs Micawber could see her husband's feathers were ruffled by Godfrey's interruption and she flashed him a warning look. Godfrey looked down sheepishly at his empty plate and muttered an apology.

'Sorry.'

As if the interruption had not mattered one jot, Micawber waved it aside magnanimously and continued admonishing his son.

'So let this be your warning, Wilkins – put your trust *only* in certainties. And on that final note of caution, I conclude my summing-up.'

With great relish, Micawber plunged the carving knife into the chicken. Even though she had not yet eaten anything, Mrs Micawber dabbed daintily at the corner of her mouth with a napkin before speaking to Godfrey.

'I have always been of the opinion that Mr Micawber, with his talent for critical examination, should have been called to the Bar.'

Making up the lost ground from the interruption *faux pas*, Godfrey nodded enthusiastically before addressing Micawber.

'You certainly have a sublime command of the English language, sir.'

Micawber looked suitably modest, but everyone could see, by the trace of a smile that tugged at the corners of his mouth, he was pleased with the compliment. It was his wife who dashed that smile from his face.

'If only,' she wailed, 'Mr Micawber could apply that talent to some pecuniary end.'

In the circumstances, Micawber thought his wife's opinion was unnecessary, especially as it was expressed in such a dismissive manner. Godfrey came to the rescue.

'Well, if you don't think it presumptuous of me to suggest, ma'am—'

Mrs Micawber, who was rather taken with the young man, smiled. 'Not at all, Master McNeil.'

'Newspapers!' Godfrey shouted excitedly. 'Melbourne already has five of its own journals, and circulation is improving. Could Mr Micawber not seek employment as a writer for the newspapers?'

Young Wilkins signalled his approval by tapping the side of his plate with a fork. 'A capital suggestion, Godfrey.'

Mr Micawber stopped carving and looked upwards as he mulled the proposition over. 'Hmm. The reportage of the news is somewhat scant and lacking when it comes to the golden language of Milton and Shakespeare. In short, they need a hack.'

'Not for feature writing, sir,' said Godfrey. 'These can be about any topical subject and are paid on a pro rata basis.'

Micawber thought briefly about this, then smiled, put down the carving knife and raised his wine glass. 'Why bless you, Master McNeil – friend and bosom companion to our family. You have saved us from extinction. You have given us hope, and given me inspiration. Let us drink to your health.'

They all raised their glasses to Godfrey, who looked pleased with himself.

'Now!' said Micawber. 'Let us ingest these fine comestibles, before they lose their genial warmth.'

8

Confusions

BY CONTRAST TO the sense of gaiety and optimism that had quickly been insinuated by young Godfrey McNeil at the Micawber meal, dinner in the Begs household was a gloomy affair.

Mr Begs sat at the top of the long dining able, while his wife sat at the opposite end, and the distance seemed to accentuate the divide that seemed to be increasing daily in their discussions about their son and marriage to Miss Micawber. Mrs Begs hated the punishing silence more than anything. She attempted to clear her throat softly, and the grinding noise caused her to wince. She gazed at her husband, hoping for Mr Begs to at least acknowledge her with some small talk. She found the silence overwhelmingly stifling and embarrassing, especially as the maid was still present, serving their dinner from tureens and platters on the sideboard. She studied her husband's expression, as he stared ominously at the table in front of him, a faraway look in his eyes, his brow lined with frown lines which grew more pronounced at every second, and she knew the anger he was holding back would soon erupt; but not while the maid was present.

Wooden floorboards creaked beneath the maid's feet as she moved a few paces nearer to her employer. She was ill at ease, unsettled by the strained atmosphere. Her eyes, fearful like a young child, indicated her discomfort as she made a half-hearted gesture towards Ridger's place-setting, wondering if she should serve his dinner.

Mr Begs pulled out his pocket watch and clicked it open. 'You can clear my son's place,' he said. 'He won't be dining with us.'

The maid nodded silently, cleared the cutlery, tugged open the sideboard drawer, and put each knife, fork and spoon away gently, in case the clatter should disturb the unholy silence. As Mr Begs watched her, he felt his impatience rattling inside him, and he opened and closed his hand as he waited. Eventually she finished her task, slid the drawer closed, and scurried from the room, relieved to escape the unpleasant atmosphere.

Mrs Begs waited for the inevitable explosion. They had begun the conversation about their son prior to dinner, but had postponed it while the maid served.

'I've spoken to Mr Larkfield,' Begs began, grabbing his knife and fork, and sawing forcefully at a portion of roast lamb, 'and he tells me the Micawbers were in a position to clear some of the arrears.' He thrust a slice of meat into his mouth, chewed angrily, then suddenly burst out, 'After I told Ridger! I expressly forbade him to bail them out.'

His wife watched with alarm as a small piece of meat was ejected from her husband's mouth and landed on the tablecloth. He waved his knife in the air to accentuate his point.

'I told him not to do it. And he's defied me.'

Mrs Begs picked up her cutlery delicately and leaned forward slightly across the divide to emphasize her point. 'But he's in love. His only concern is for Emma's welfare. And perhaps we should be encouraging this union. She's an intelligent girl. Ridger needs someone like her. It's his only hope.'

Begs scowled and attacked his dinner. 'What's that supposed to mean?'

'Well, I love him dearly, but I have no illusions concerning his abilities.'

She could see her husband was about to speak and continued hastily, 'Admittedly, when he is in certain company, he surpasses himself; and when it comes to masculine pursuits such as hunting

59

and riding – well – he knows how to take care of himself. But he is really rather a baby.'

Mr Begs snorted dismissively. 'You mean he's spoilt.'

'It's understandable. An only child.'

Begs glanced at his wife, and then focused on his dinner. The lack of another child brought out all his insecurities. Most men in his position would have blamed their spouse, but Begs realized that the weakness or blame could as easily lie at his own door.

'I mean,' Mrs Begs added, 'an only child gets all the attention and doesn't feel a need to compete for the parents' approval.'

'That,' Begs snapped, jabbing the air with his fork, 'is all the more reason for my not giving in to him over this Micawber business.'

Mrs Begs, about to eat a small morsel balanced on the end of her fork, stopped and protested. 'But surely a compromise ...'

Her husband waved it aside impatiently. 'I don't see why I should be expected to compromise my principles. You know my feelings concerning the likes of the Micawbers.'

'Yes, *I* know your reasons, but Ridger doesn't. Perhaps if he did, it might…. Isn't it time you told him? You can't keep your past from your son forever.'

Begs stopped eating and frowned thoughtfully. 'We'll see.'

Mrs Begs smiled involuntarily, knowing her husband had given a slight indication that he might not be entirely rigid over this business. Having toyed with her food up until now, she suddenly found her appetite and began eating.

While Agnes cleared the table, Mr and Mrs Micawber and Young Wilkins stood behind Godfrey, who had made himself comfortable on the piano stool and was flexing his fingers.

'I think we are all familiar with the works of Mr Robert Herrick,' he said.

Micawber nodded enthusiastically. 'Indeed, indeed! "Cherry Ripe" being an excruciatingly affectionate ballad which has gladdened the heart in many a parlour.' He patted Godfrey's shoulder. '*Con anima, con brio*, young Godfrey.'

Godfrey paused, his hands suspended over the keys, and looked up at Micawber. 'I'm not exactly familiar ...'

Micawber smiled as he explained, 'With deep feeling and with vigour.'

Godfrey returned his smile. 'Indeed, sir.'

In one fluid movement, Godfrey's hands caressed the keyboard and the introduction sprang to life. Mr Micawber's eyes became glassy with sentiment and his voice boomed harmonically as he launched into the song with relish. Young Wilkins, perhaps over-shadowed by his father, began a trifle faintly, but soon sang out with gusto as he gained confidence. Mrs Micawber, smiling beat-ifically, luxuriated in the lusty baritone of husband and son, and waited until the second phrase before joining in, and she had no sooner enhanced the song with a piercing vibrato when the door was flung open by Emma Micawber, whose expression of confu-sion gave her the appearance of a startled fawn. Thinking her family was in the throes of eviction, she was shocked to find them singing harmoniously around the piano. Godfrey, reacting to her entrance like someone struck by an uplifting ray of sunshine, stopped playing.

'Ah! My Turtle Dove,' Micawber began. 'You are just in time to—'

'Mama! Papa!' gasped Emma. 'What is happening?'

With an elegant circular gesture, her father waved a hand at Godfrey, saying, 'Allow me to introduce you to Master Godfrey McNeil – a newly acquainted but thoroughly accorded friend of the Micawber household. This is our daughter, Miss Emma Micawber.'

Godfrey rose from the piano stool and gave Emma a small bow. 'If I may be permitted to speak openly, it is indeed a great honour to meet one whose enchantment fills the room, and augments the already ...' – he paused and looked towards Mr and then Mrs Micawber – 'cultured and elegant company.'

Godfrey waited for the excellent response he now felt was his due from the startlingly attractive daughter. Instead, her face crumpled and she burst into tears.

'Words!' she cried. 'More words! More meaningless words!'

Her sudden departure from the room, slamming the door as she went, created an embarrassed and thoroughly confused silence. Godfrey was the first to break it.

'I hope there was no impropriety—' he began.

Micawber clapped him on the back. 'Of course not, Master Godfrey. Please don't hold yourself accountable. She is suffering from a malady of the heart.'

Godfrey stared at the door, wishing he was the object of her affections.

Thomas and Amelia Begs had almost finished their meal when Ridger walked into the leaden atmosphere of the dining room, bearing a sullen, pouting expression. His face was flushed and his eyes were glassy, and it looked as if he might have been drinking. His father avoided eye contact, clattered his knife and fork together, sat back in his dining chair, and drummed the fingers of one hand upon the table, a gesture that indicated an impatient desire for some sort of explanation of his son's behaviour.

Ridger glowered at the back of his father's head while his mother stated the obvious.

'Ridger, you've missed dinner.'

'I'm not hungry.'

'I hope you haven't been drinking.'

Ridger stared at his mother defiantly. 'What if I have?'

Banging the table with his fist, Thomas Begs snapped, 'Don't speak that way to your mother.' He turned to glare at his son. 'Sit down! I want a word with you.'

Ridger half turned towards the door. 'I don't think there's much point—'

Begs banged his fist down again, this time twice as hard, so that the crockery jumped. 'Sit down!' he yelled. 'And listen to what I have to say.'

His mother looked at him pleadingly. 'Please, Ridger.'

With a show of reluctance, Ridger sank into a chair, turning slightly away from his father, like a spoilt and sulky child. His father stared at him for a moment, his brow furrowed, as he wondered where to begin. He cleared his throat softly before speaking.

'Ridger, you know so little about me; about the past and my life in England. Have you never been curious about my history?'

Feeling uncomfortable, Ridger shifted in his chair. 'Well, I suppose ...'

'Perhaps it is my fault,' Begs continued. 'I have been evasive. Perhaps we should have spoken about my past many years ago.'

'What has this to do with the Micawbers?'

'Listen to me, Ridger: I should have spoken to you about this before now, so that you could understand how I feel about the Micawbers. But now I will tell you something about my life back in England, when I was a child. My father was a wealthy landowner, and we lived in one of the largest houses in the county of Kent. And one day, as if having awoken from a dream about some sort of utopian ideal, he became a highly principled human being. He had always been a kind and generous man, but one day he began putting certain beliefs into practice, fostering a faith in social equality. He took pity on the poor; fed and clothed them, and gave them a home. He entertained noble ideas about the redistribution of wealth. But they just took everything he owned, giving nothing in return. Not even their loyalty. The money ran out, and so did they. Disillusioned, and almost penniless, my father drank himself to death, leaving my mother and me to the meagre charity of the parish.'

Frowning deeply, with an open-mouthed look of bewilderment that always irritated his mother, Ridger turned towards his father. 'I still don't understand....'

'Your father is worried,' said Mrs Begs.

'What about?'

'He's worried the Micawbers will destroy him in the same way that his father was destroyed.'

Begs shook his head vigorously. 'That's putting it strongly. Much too strongly. But I want you, Ridger, to understand how I feel about the Micawbers. They are like the people who bled my father dry. The Micawbers of this world take advantage of the goodwill of others and they need to understand that. And now they will always expect financial aid, since you have provided them with assistance and paid their rent for them.'

'I don't understand,' Ridger said. 'I didn't give them any money.'

'Don't lie to me, Ridger. I have spoken with Mr Larkfield, who informs me that they've paid half the arrears.'

'Not with my money, they haven't. I still have it. I tried to persuade Emma to take it, but she refused. I can't think why.'

As Begs stared at Ridger, he realized his son was incapable of deception. He may be headstrong, disobedient and excitable, but he was always open and honest.

'I knew Emma Micawber was an intelligent girl,' Mrs Begs offered.

Nonplussed, Begs looked towards his wife. 'Then who was it bailed them out?'

Ridger, angered as much by his own confusion as what he considered an unfair charge, pointed an accusatory finger at his father. 'Well, of one thing we can be certain, it wasn't you.' He pushed his chair away from the table and rose. 'Now if you'll excuse me....'

Both palms turned upwards, a gesture of supplication, Begs said, 'If it is any consolation, Ridger, I am deeply glad they have found the means with which to avoid further financial embarrassment.'

Eyes blazing, Ridger stared hard into his father's eyes. 'And I deeply regret that it was not my father who helped them out.'

He swung round and stormed out of the room. An uncomfortable silence prevailed as Begs stared helplessly into the distance. His wife moved to sit nearer him, in the chair vacated by Ridger.

'You ought to have told him everything,' she said.

Begs shook his head uncertainly, and his wife saw the hurt and the fear in his eyes. She placed a hand gently over his.

'Thomas, I know how much you're afraid of emulating your father but—'

'That's half the trouble,' Begs broke in. 'In a way I have great admiration for what he did. But I can't help despising the ingrates, those leeches who sucked him dry.'

Mrs Begs squeezed his hand. 'But you can't go on tormenting yourself. You must let it rest now. It happened such a long time ago, in another life. You must bury it once and for all.'

Begs thought about this for a moment, and then appeared to relax. 'As long as Ridger realizes that when they get married, he may have to support the in-laws as well.'

Surprised and pleased, Mrs Begs smiled. 'Did you say *when* they get married?' She saw the teasing glint in her husband's eyes. 'Oh, Thomas, I do love you.'

She rose, came and stood close to him, leaned over and kissed him full on the lips. As the maid entered to clear the dinner plates, she broke away like a startled rabbit.

9

Reflections on a Strange Continent

PAPER SURROUNDED MR Micawber as he scratched away at yet another clean sheet which lay before him on the parlour table. Each dip of his pen into the inkwell gave him a sense of optimism and there would be a surge in his endeavours, and an even greater improvement in his creative efforts. But the inspiration he so dearly sought eluded him. Out of the corner of his eye he could see the figure of Young Wilkins standing near the piano, posing and gesturing, and he used this distraction as an excuse to end his search for innovation. He threw down his pen dramatically.

'Alas!' he intoned. 'The inspiration has deserted me.'

Young Wilkins stopped in mid gesture, an arm raised as if to fend off an imaginary assailant, and turned to address his father.

'I never thought I should live to see that day.'

Mr Micawber sighed deeply before replying. 'It is the influence of this strange continent. Birds which never fly; strange beasts that hop about with their offspring in their pockets. Where are the babbling brooks and lofty oaks? I fear had Keats been born in this strange land, the world would be the poorer for poetry.'

Young Wilkins abandoned his pose, thrust his hands into his pockets and leaned nonchalantly against the side of the piano.

'But you are writing newspaper articles,' he stressed. 'Not verses.'

Micawber dismissed it with a wave of the hand. 'Even so, they must have literary merit. But I fear the Muse has flown.'

Young Wilkins, staring pointedly at the abundance of paper spread across the table, said, 'But not before she inspired you to complete six volumes, it appears.'

'I intend to be prolific, thus increasing the chances of publication.'

'It was unfortunate that none of the editors was responsive.'

Thoughtfully, Micawber ran a hand across the shiny baldness of his head. 'Newspaper editors are renowned for being literal, unimaginative and commonplace. If I may sound immodest for a moment, I thought my article about the Noble Savage was unsurpassed.'

Young Wilkins shook his head dismissively. 'The indigenous population is a sticky topic.'

Suddenly, as a thought struck him, Young Wilkins hurriedly left the room, then reappeared seconds later, opening the door wide to signal a lavish entrance, his chest puffed out. He closed the door without looking back, and strutted towards the piano, bowing low to an imaginary person. His father observed these antics with a faintly amused glint in his eye.

'Er – might one enquire as to the purpose of this strange exhibition?'

'I have to practise entrances, exits, sitting, standing, bowing and gesturing.'

'Ah! You are still determined to pursue the profession of actor then? Have I ever shown you my Othello?'

'Yes!' Young Wilkins said quickly.

Rather too quickly, thought his father.

'But shouldn't you be trying to summon back the Muse? Another week and Mr Begs's agent may return.'

Micawber looked towards the window, as if the outside world was to blame for his misfortune. Another long sigh before he spoke.

'It is indeed sad how Mr Begs has devoted his life to the worship of Mammon.'

'On the contrary, Papa, he seeks fame in horse racing.'

'Ah! The sport of kings.'

'It is his one consuming passion, almost to the point of obsession.'

Micawber stared thoughtfully at his writing tools, and an idea began to form, almost as if he could see words magically dancing across paper. After a brief pause, he looked towards his son with a faint trace of a smile. 'Really? How interesting.'

But Young Wilkins hadn't noticed the change in his father's mood, and was more concerned with resuming his posturing. Suddenly, like a coiled spring unwinding, he exited extravagantly, looking over his shoulder as he left the room and slammed the door.

Micawber, who was now struck hard by his idea, smacked his hands together and rose excitedly. 'Wilkins!' he cried. 'The Muse has returned.'

After waiting a moment for his son's next entrance, he grew impatient and dashed over to the door. When he threw it open, expecting to see his Young Wilkins collecting himself prior to another dramatic entrance, he found himself gazing at the silence of the hallway. Young Wilkins had vanished. It had clearly been a genuine exit.

'Oh!' was all Micawber could manage. But his disappointment at being unable to share his great idea was momentary and he hurried back to his table. He dipped his pen in the ink and began writing furiously, his tongue protruding from his mouth like a child's as ideas flashed before him.

10

A Drama Lesson

SEARCHING FOR HIS friend Godfrey in Canvas Town was rather like searching for a needle in a haystack, thought Young Wilkins, as he trudged the still muddy tracks between rows of tents. There must have been at least a thousand of these temporary migrant homes, the sleeping quarters of young men drawn to Melbourne by the lure of gold in 1851. No wonder prices were so astronomical, with traders being able to charge what they liked.

A stream of sweat ran down from the nape of Young Wilkins's neck to the small of his back, and his shirt clung to his body. The continuous blast of hot wind from the west was like a breath from hell itself.

He waved his arms about like a mad man to ward off the mosquitoes which bombarded him, unconcerned by how he must look to the inhabitants of Canvas Town, whose main concerns were in finding employment, or raising the money for a licence to dig for gold.

As he stumbled along the rutted tracks, head bent low and arms waving frantically like a demented windmill, and occasionally almost barging into tent dwellers, he struggled to recognize any landmark that would offer a clue as to his friend's whereabouts. He had been to Canvas Town only once before to visit Godfrey and he knew his friend had been fortunate enough to find accommodation in a shack, rather than a tent, which belonged to a young Welshman who had gone to seek his fortune with the discovery of gold at Mount Korong. Godfrey had promised to look after it for him in case his digging resulted in failure.

Weaving between tents, and stepping carefully over guy ropes, he suddenly remembered his friend's shack was close to a grog shanty, a rather basic public house, on which someone had humorously painted The Royal Oak in white above the door. Turning into another long alleyway of tents, he spotted the makeshift shanty that looked as if it would not resist the next gust of wind; and, as he got closer to the ramshackle building, he saw its identifying misnomer over the door. Just beyond that he counted six more tents, and then he came to a small shack, no bigger than a garden shed. He knocked twice on the door and waited. He heard a scuffling sound from within, and then Godfrey's voice asked, 'Who is it?'

'It's me, your friend Wilkins Micawber.'

Another sound from inside the shack, as if untidiness was being hastily rectified, and then Young Wilkins heard a bolt clanking across on the inside, the door swung open and he found himself staring at a figure in a black mask.

'Ah, Wilkins! My dear chap!' Godfrey's voice was muffled by a veil.

'I recognize the voice, even though the face seems unfamiliar,' Young Wilkins said.

'It's these parasitical creatures. All that rain and now the heat: a fateful combination. These mosquitoes will be the death of me. Come in, Young Wilkins. Come in.'

Once inside the gloomy shack, which only had one small window about a foot square, Young Wilkins recognized the small camp bed from his previous visit, a tea chest for a table, and other sundry boxes to use as chairs. Up against the wall under the tiny window was a solid chest, securely fastened with a padlock.

Godfrey made sure he had shut the door before removing his veil. He grinned at his friend and pointed to his own face. 'Not too many bites, you see. But without the veil I would look like a child with chicken pox.'

Young Wilkins cast his eyes around the gloomy shack. 'No mosquitoes in here, Godfrey; yet you were wearing the veil indoors.'

'I was just on my way out. I was going to St. Kilda for some sea-bathing. I can thoroughly recommend it. It's both healthy and invigorating.'

'But I can't swim.'

Godfrey chuckled. 'Oh, just to immerse oneself in seawater is sufficiently pleasurable. I go at least three times a week.'

'I'll give it serious consideration.' Young Wilkins touched his own jaw, which had started to itch, and he wondered how badly he had been bitten.

'Don't scratch those bites, my dear chap,' Godfrey advised. 'You'll only make it worse. Best to leave well alone.'

'I suppose I'd better get myself a veil if I'm to survive this climate. And my appearance may prove to be vital.'

Godfrey raised his eyebrows as he stared questioningly at his friend, waiting for him to elaborate.

'For some time now, Godfrey, I've been performing comic songs, and I've managed to gain a certain confidence in the performing arts. I have also been studying the Bard of Avon, and now I truly believe that my chosen calling is in the theatre. I have decided to become an actor.'

Godfrey scowled, almost as if he had been insulted, and Young Wilkins, who had an almost childish expectation of his friend's encouraging response, felt as if he had been slapped.

'Is something the matter?' he asked.

Godfrey's scowl uncoiled and he forced a smile, though it lacked sincerity. 'Oh, I knew someone in London who had high expectations of becoming an actor.' His eyes became wistful and distant as he thought about the past. 'There were many others with the same presumptions, but this man I knew had an exceptional talent and was offered a variety of roles with a company touring on the outskirts of London and many other theatres in the Home Counties. For weeks he learnt many roles in several dramas, with the manager promising him an extravagant salary once a performance week had ended with some hopefully lucrative box-office receipts.'

Godfrey broke off, and his face clouded with anger as he fought some distant conflict.

'What happened?' Young Wilkins prompted.

'At the end of the second week the manager vanished with the takings, leaving the actor destitute.'

'What did he do?'

Godfrey shook his head, indicating that he wished to say nothing further on the subject. 'It doesn't matter.'

A silence ensued, and Young Wilkins was aware of the uncomfortable oven-like heat inside the hut as the sun scalded the roof mercilessly.

'Thank you for telling me that story,' he said after a long pause, 'which will assist me in being on my guard for rogues and vagabonds in that profession, for I fully intend to pursue this worthy calling.'

Godfrey, who appeared to be only half-listening to his friend's innocent ambitions, suddenly shrugged off his dark mood, and offered his friend a toothy grin.

'Very well then, Young Wilkins. Allow me to see something of your expertise in the art of treading the boards.'

'I don't follow you.'

'That is what we— that was what my thespian friend called acting. The boards are the wooden stages of theatres.'

'Yes, of course. But surely you don't want me to perform for you in here?'

'Why not?'

Young Wilkins raised his arms uncertainly. 'Well, this stifling heat.'

'Come, come, Young Wilkins! If your heart is set on performing in this country, then you will need to become acclimatized to the discomfort of performing in these conditions.'

'But why do you wish to see me perform?'

'I might be able to offer you some advice.'

Young Wilkins's eyes narrowed as he studied his friend. 'This so-called friend of yours, in the mother country, would this by any chance be your good self?'

Before answering, Godfrey broke eye contact with Young Wilkins. 'Perish the thought! I have never been an actor.'

'Then why do you wish to offer me advice?'

'Because I spent much of my youth visiting the theatre, and have become something of an expert. Almost a critic, you might say.'

'You have never told me, Godfrey, what occupation you served in London.'

'I was a lowly clerk in a law firm. And I came to this country hoping to better myself. Now then, Wilkins, let me see how you can breathe life into one of Mr Shakespeare's creations.'

Young Wilkins shifted nervously from one foot to the other. 'Um – er—'

'I'm here to help, Wilkins. I will encourage and assist you. What's it to be?'

'Um – I thought I might perform the Hamlet soliloquy from act one, scene two.'

Godfrey clapped his hands together enthusiastically. 'An excellent choice!'

He watched as Young Wilkins prepared himself, pulling himself proudly upright, and holding the back of his hand to his forehead.

'"Oh",' Young Wilkins intoned, '"that this too, too solid flesh should melt, thaw and—"'

'Just a minute!' Godfrey said.

Young Wilkins was nonplussed by the interruption. His hand, held so positively aloft in a tragic pose, withered on the vine.

'What's wrong?' he snapped.

Godfrey knew he had to tread carefully, so as not to damage a frail ego. 'Your hand,' he said.

'What about it?'

'Tell me why you are holding it thus?'

Godfrey demonstrated.

'Hamlet is in a tragic mood, having suffered the loss of his father, and his mother is marrying his brother so soon—'

'Yes, yes, yes!' Godfrey said. 'But explain to me why the hand has to be in that position. Have you ever been truly depressed? And when you were in that state – think carefully before you answer – did you hold your hand to your forehead like that?'

Young Wilkins frowned as he thought about it. 'No, I don't think I did.'

'Well then, why do you think Hamlet does it?'

There was a long, frowning pause while Young Wilkins considered it. 'I think drama has a particular style. It is not nature. It goes above and beyond nature and—'

'Sorry to interrupt you,' Godfrey said, 'but what you are doing is imitating what other actors think is a style they should be adopting. All they are doing is copying each other. Don't you see, once you start making gestures like that, your character's energy is dissipated, so that it becomes harder for the audience to hear the words. Start the speech again, and instead of using a gesture that other actors have used to denote tragedy, try to feel inwardly the man's confusion and suffering. Think about the words – only that.'

Young Wilkins stood awkwardly, his frame suddenly wooden. He began the speech again, his hands knotted together for the opening two lines; but as soon as he reached the word 'everlasting', his hands shot up in the air, as if he were embracing the Almighty.

'I'm going to stop you again,' Godfrey said. He could see Young Wilkins was becoming thoroughly demoralized and added hastily, 'It was much, much better up until "everlasting". Couldn't you feel it yourself?'

'Well, actually no. I felt the words needed punctuating with a gesture of some sort.'

Stifling a sigh, Godfrey said, 'Do not forget, Wilkins, these are a man's thoughts. They need no demonstration. The audience wants to hear the man's thoughts; they don't want to see him acting them. Please try it once more from the beginning and really just think about what you are saying. Then I will be able to see your thoughts clearly and there will be no need for you to demonstrate with gestures. This time I won't interrupt you.'

Young Wilkins nodded, took a deep breath and thought about the opening lines and their meaning. And then, as he started to speak slowly and thoughtfully, Godfrey saw the transformation taking place. He was witnessing a rebirth, as Young Wilkins got into his stride, resisted any posturing gestures, concentrating instead on the way the words affected his conflicting emotions. By the time he had reached the end of the speech, with the sweat running from his forehead, he was exhausted by the internal force of Hamlet's contradictions.

He turned to look towards Godfrey, desperately seeking approval.

'Bravo!' Godfrey said with a gentle smile. 'That was excellent. Could you feel how much better that was?'

Young Wilkins nodded effusively. He seemed awed by what he had learnt. 'Up until now,' he whispered, 'I realize I was just posturing. But that is all behind me. A great change has taken place and my eyes have been opened. And I have you to thank for that, Godfrey.'

Godfrey laughed and patted his friend's arm. 'I'm sure you'll go from strength to strength, my dear chap.'

'I find it incredible that you were able to instruct me knowing exactly what was required. Now don't try to tell me you have no performing experience yourself, Godfrey, because I don't feel inclined to believe you.'

Godfrey's eyes shifted from his friend's probing gaze. 'I suppose I did dabble, but merely as an amateur. And, as I think I may have mentioned, I saw many plays on the London stage. Now then, you seem to be perspiring profusely. If I can find you something to wear, why not join me for a spot of sea-bathing?'

11

The Sport of Kings

HURRYING ALONG COLLINS Street to the offices of the *Melbourne Chronicle*, and carrying a sheaf of papers which he clutched protectively to his chest, Mr Micawber halted briefly to gaze longingly into the window of a wine merchant. His optimism was at low ebb. Several times he had made this self-same visit to the newspaper office, and several times he had peered expectantly into this self-same window, only to have his hopes dashed with the rejection of his articles.

Perhaps his latest endeavour stood more chance of a publication. Not one for being weighed down or blighted by pessimism, he drew himself up to his full height and strutted hopefully into the office of the *Melbourne Chronicle*.

It was a small outer office, with a counter for the submission of Classified Advertisements. There was an archway leading to a large office with many desks, at which sat reporters silently scratching away laboriously, hunched over their stories, as if guarding them from would-be plagiarists. Next to the archway leading to the reporters' room, was a small untidy office belonging to the editor. The door remained permanently open so that he was always aware of the comings and goings of his staff.

As he caught sight of Micawber with yet another one of his lengthy articles, his face remained inscrutably calm, but the monotone of his voice betrayed a distinct lack of interest.

'Ah, Mr Micawber,' he said, as he got up from his desk and came into the outer office. 'It's you again.'

Like a Regency dandy, Micawber swept an arm across his ample stomach and bowed low. 'Your servant, sir.'

Irritated by this excessive display, the editor brushed it away with a flick of his hand. 'Never mind all that.' He nodded at the sheaf of papers. 'What have you been writing this time? Not another anecdote about the time you accidentally bumped into the Archbishop of Canterbury.'

'I swear upon the King James, the Koran or any other holy book, that every word was true.'

'I've no doubt. But ten thousand words on the subject was just a wee bit long, I thought.'

Unperturbed by the criticism, Micawber handed his article to the editor with a flourish. 'I think that when you read this, you will be – to coin a phrase from one of our pugilistic diversions – well and truly floored.'

Reluctantly, the editor took the papers and glanced at the top sheet. Micawber watched him as his eyes flicked speedily along the opening sentence, and then shifted downwards, to and fro, taking it in at a rapid rate. While Micawber waited, he heard a raucous laugh and a cough from the main office, and wheels clattering out in the street. His nose was tickled by the slight feeling of sawdust floating in the stagnant air. As the editor turned to the second page, Micawber's spirits were raised.

'Horse racing, eh? Very interesting. Hmm – yes. Mr Begs seems to figure greatly in the theme of this article.'

Micawber nodded effusively. 'Understandably. Mr Begs is the Leonardo of equestrianism. Arab steeds kowtow to his commands; Welsh ponies dance to his every whim; he can make Shire horses fly like dainty gazelles. In short, he is a talented trainer of horses.'

The editor stared at Micawber, his eyes narrowing shrewdly. 'And, in short, you know which side your bread is buttered. Now then, Mr Micawber, our rates are one farthing per word....'

Micawber took a step back, his face a mixture of surprise and delight. 'You wish to publish it?'

'It will go in the next edition.'

Micawber, brows furrowed, tried to do some hasty mental arithmetic. 'Er – three thousand, two hundred and six words – um – four farthings to the penny – that's um – not quite one thousand pennies. That's...um—'

'That is why,' the editor broke in impatiently, 'it will be edited down to a more realistic size. If you return this afternoon, I should be able to let you have a proof and payment. Good-day, Mr Micawber.'

'And good-day to you, Mr Kynoch,' Micawber replied, as he backed away towards the door, beaming unsparingly. 'This is just the beginning! The beginning!' He doffed his hat before leaving.

The editor watched him exit into the chaos and congestion of Collins Street, then raised his eyes towards the ceiling and muttered, 'I think your reputation is safe, Sir Walter.'

He called one of the reporters from the main office and handed him Micawber's article. 'Cut this down to fifteen hundred words and let me see it. I want it in the next edition.'

The reporter, weasel-faced, with perhaps a dozen strands of ginger hair combed sideways in a vain attempt to hide his baldness, took the papers and scratched his chin. 'Out of all the articles he's submitted, you've accepted this one. Why?'

'Because never was a man like Thomas Begs singled out for so much praise, and I'm in an evil frame of mind. It'll put that damned Shelbourne's nose out of joint.'

The reporter sniggered, 'Since when did Captain Shelbourne merit such treatment?'

'You know as well as I do, Sam. Since the captain accused me of concocting that story about the new treasury building last year.'

'He'd been drinking, so I hear.'

The editor shuddered at the memory. 'That doesn't excuse such bad behaviour at a public function. So I think Mr Begs and his horses could do with a little hyperbolic praise.'

The reporter grinned at his employer and started to read through the article. Whistling softly, the editor returned to his office.

12

The Next Edition

BEGS PUSHED HIS breakfast plate to one side, picked up his newspaper and began reading. His wife sipped her tea, and stared at Ridger's empty place, a slightly puzzled expression on her face.

'I know we've had words with Ridger over the Micawbers, but I thought it was resolved. It isn't like him to disappear without informing me.'

Begs shrugged as his eyes scanned the front page. 'I heard him leaving in the early hours, just before dawn.' Turning over a page, he explained to his wife, 'I see he's taken the dogs. So he must have gone ...'

His voice trailed off as something in the paper caught his eye. Lost in her own thoughts concerning her son, Mrs Begs didn't notice how caught up her husband was with the article he was reading.

'I only hope Ridger remembers that he's taking tea with Emma Micawber this afternoon. They are *such* an ideal match. What a pity her father is not.' She put down her cup and addressed her husband. 'Have you reached a decision yet about Mr Micawber?'

She jumped slightly as Begs brought the paper down with a crackle. He handed her the article to read as he got up from the table.

'Yes. I think it is high time Mr Micawber paid me a visit.'

His wife looked worried as she began reading the article, and her husband strode purposefully towards the door.

With the exception of Emma, who had excused herself to attend to her toiletries, the Micawber family was gathered around the breakfast table, listening carefully to the reading of the article about horse racing. Mr Micawber strung out every word with relish, while his wife listened intently, her head slightly cocked, and a delicate smile displayed the correct degree of pride for her husband's achievement. Young Wilkins, on the other hand, frowned hard, and it was unclear whether his features revealed concentration or disapproval. The twins, Emily and Edward, eyes wide as they concentrated and tried to understand the verbal skills of their father, leaned forward across the table, their expressions rich with attentiveness. As Micawber reached the final paragraph of his article, his voice grew in intensity.

'… this chestnut symmetrical god, that Poseidon himself must have fashioned on Mount Olympus, and is *nonpareil* on the turf….'

'What does *nonpareil* mean, Papa?' Emily interrupted.

Mrs Micawber made a show of putting a finger to her mouth to shush her daughter, but Micawber waved the interruption aside magnanimously, and lowered his paper to address his daughter.

'It means he has no equal. Um – where was I?' He raised his paper again and his eyes strained to focus on the place. 'Ah yes: "and is *nonpareil* on the turf, is certain to make Mr Thomas Begs the *king* of the sport of kings. Wilkins Micawber, Esquire".'

He put the paper down and looked around the table for approval. There was a ripple of applause from everyone except Young Wilkins, who still frowned thoughtfully. His father noticed his lack of enthusiasm and raised his eyebrows questioningly.

'How is it,' demanded Young Wilkins, 'this horse has no equal when it hasn't even raced yet?'

Micawber smiled a trifle patronizingly and explained carefully, 'This racehorse is, I believe – if I may descend for a moment to the jargon of the turf – a dead cert!'

Young Wilkins shook his head in disbelief. 'Well, if I was Thomas Begs, and read that article, I should be exceedingly displeased.'

'How so?'

'It might make the horse so popular that the odds will diminish. And if Mr Begs is a betting man....'

Young Wilkins let his incomplete sentence hang in the air like a portent of doom, while his father looked concerned. And at that precise moment there was a knock upon their front door. They waited in silence as they listened to Agnes answering it. Presently she entered the living room and presented Micawber with a note.

'There's a man at the door, says 'e's got to wait for a reply.'

Frowning, Micawber read the note, while everyone waited expectantly. After a moment, he looked up and explained worriedly, 'It's from Mr Begs. He wishes to see me at my earliest convenience.'

Having agreed to meet Thomas Begs later that morning, Mr Micawber spent the remaining time as he waited for the carriage that was arranged to collect him, scribbling another newspaper article about fate, and how much luck played its part in selecting winners or losers. He hoped Mr Kynoch would publish the article, which might make amends for the praise he had heaped on Mr Begs's most treasured horse.

13

Lost for Words

DURING THE JOURNEY that morning, Mr Micawber suffered imaginary torments and tortures for having lowered the odds on Mr Begs's horses and, as the carriage pulled up in front of his landlord's estate, Micawber felt a lump in his throat the size of plum stone. He was directed by one of the servants around the side of the house to the stables at the rear.

He set off with great trepidation, walking delicately, almost on tiptoe, as if he was treading on hallowed ground. He passed a large kitchen garden, and crept along a short path near several barns, until he came upon the stables, where he spotted Begs, affectionately cuddling and stroking the blaze of a large grey mare.

Surely, thought Micawber, a man given to such displays of affection to an animal might have a little drop of human kindness to spare for a fellow creature, however unworthy. But, for once, Micawber was aware of his shortcomings, and his optimism had deserted him in his hour of need. His hopes were dashed! He dreaded this confrontation, and wished he had a trump card with which to astound his landlord. He knew in his heart of hearts that another piece of writing on horse racing, following closely on the previous article, would prove to be undesirable as far as Mr Kynoch was concerned.

Micawber stared at Begs's broad shoulders as he nervously approached, wondering if the man was given to fisticuffs if driven to extremes. He dismissed the foreboding as nonsense. Begs had never given him that impression, so why now was Micawber's judgement becoming clouded by such internal ramblings? Aware that his fear was causing him to exaggerate his peril, he chased the pessimism from his mind and summoned up a last gasp of sanguinity.

'Good-day!' he hollered.

Begs spun round, his expression one of sheer alarm. 'Mr Micawber! You startled me. I wasn't expecting you quite so soon.'

Micawber doubted this was true, else why would his landlord have sent a carriage to pick him up? In spite of this misgiving, Micawber produced his sincerest expression, and placed a hand on his heart. 'The brevity of your note left me in no doubt as to its urgency. So I came with rapid strides!'

'I hope you did not leave any business unattended on my account.'

Missing this slight note of sarcasm, Micawber replied, 'If I say I downed tools in order to be here, I am merely being metaphorically excessive. There was no pressing business.'

Giving his horse a final pat on its nose, Begs walked several paces away from the stall, and turned to face Micawber.

'Then I think we can get straight to the point, Mr Micawber. My passion for horses and your new career in journalism: you seem to have taken it upon yourself to make my business your business.'

Micawber felt that hard lump in his throat again. 'I – I can explain.'

Begs waved it aside. 'There is no need. I am more than pleased with the article you wrote.'

'You – you see, when I wrote it, I did not truly comprehend,' Micawber burbled, and then stopped when he realized what his landlord had said. His eyes grew wide with this revelation. 'Pleased! Did you say *pleased*?'

Begs nodded. 'Publicity, Mr Micawber! That's what I need. Publicity! I intend to have the finest stables this side of the globe, and even though I am not unknown in Melbourne, your public tribute has created a greater awareness of my equestrian and racing ambitions. And I have estimated that had I paid for this service you have done me, it would have cost – well, shall we say it cancels your arrears and gives you a month's free accommodation. What do you say to that?'

Micawber's mouth opened and closed like a fish several times before he spoke. 'I – I don't know what to say. I—'

Begs almost smiled. 'Mr Micawber! Don't tell me you are lost for words?'

Micawber suddenly became animated, and his eyes were moist as he shook Thomas Begs's hand in gratitude.

14

A Betrothal

IN THE MICAWBER parlour, a bumble bee buzzed angrily as it attempted to find the opening in the window, hurling itself with a plop against the pane. Neither Emma Micawber nor Ridger Begs was aware of its existence; Emma because she sat at the piano, giving an adequate rendition of *Für Elise*, and Ridger because he was lost in thought.

It was a blisteringly hot day and Emma struggled to remain controlled and poised during this spontaneous performance, brought about because Ridger had been more taciturn than usual. She ignored the salty taste of unladylike sweat running down her face, and concentrated on the last few bars of her recital. As soon as she had finished playing, she turned towards Ridger, who sat on a hard-backed chair close to her piano stool. She could see he was miles away.

'Does my playing have such a soporific effect on you, my darling?'

His face registered that something had entered his brain, although she could see it didn't amount to a complete understanding.

'Hmm?' he questioned. 'Oh, I'm sorry. I was thinking.'

Emma smiled tolerantly. 'Yes, I could see that. Anything you might wish to share with me?'

'I was thinking about Father.'

Emma's smile grew warmer. 'He has been extremely generous and kind.'

'Has he? It seems to me it was a business arrangement. If your father had not written that article—'

With a shake of the head, Emma interrupted him. 'But don't you see, Ridger, that article was the opportunity for which your father was waiting? He didn't make Papa feel it was an act of charity. Papa was able to retain his pride, and that is very important.' She took hold of his hand in order to emphasize her point. 'It was a very intelligent thing your father did, Ridger.'

With his free hand, Ridger smacked his forehead. 'I just didn't realize. I could kick myself. But how could you see it so clearly, whereas I—'

Emma squeezed his hand sympathetically. 'My sweet, darling, funny little Ridger.'

Ridger gazed at her for a while. When he spoke there was a tremor in his voice. 'Emma, now that everything seems – well – what I mean to say is, I think—'

He broke off as Emma giggled.

'Yes, Ridger! The answer is yes.'

'How did you know what I was going to say?'

Emma laughed and held both his hands. 'I know you, Ridger.'

Suddenly Ridger's face lit up with joy. 'And the answer is yes?'

'Until death us do part.'

Excited and animated, Ridger let go of her hands and stood up. 'We could make it official – announce it on Friday. Oh, there is one other thing....'

Smiling, Emma rose and took his hands in hers again. 'Ridger! You naughty boy! I suppose you want to kiss me now.'

'Do I?' For a moment Ridger looked confused, but recovered quickly. 'Oh! Yes! Yes, of course I do.'

He leaned forward, anticipating the touch of their lips, when suddenly the door was thrown open as the twins burst into the room, followed by Mrs Micawber.

Edward sniggered. 'Caught you! Ridger was going to kiss Emma. Weren't you, Ridger?'

'Oh, do be quiet, Edward, there's a good boy,' Mrs Micawber said, noticing how flushed the young couple had become.

'Will you play something for us, Emma?' Emily asked, thus saving the lovers from further embarrassment. 'Will you? Please, Emma, please.'

Mrs Micawber smiled encouragingly at her daughter. 'It is improving with each performance, My Pet.'

With a knowing glance at her betrothed, Emma resumed her seat at the piano. 'Very well. I shall play it once more.'

They all sat down and watched and listened as Emma began her second recital of *Für Elise*. She played it perfectly this time. Her performance had suddenly reached a higher level.

Mrs Micawber gave Ridger a sidelong glance and noticed how pleased he looked with himself. She guessed what had happened and secretly rejoiced at this most fortuitous union between the Micawber and Begs family.

15

Interruptions

ALTHOUGH THE PART of Prince Hal in *Henry IV Part Two* was hardly appropriate for his age, nevertheless Micawber had chosen to entertain the assembled company with the speech where the young prince assumes the throne from his dying father, and crowns himself King of England.

It was early Friday evening, and Micawber stood in the centre of the parlour – Centre Stage, as it were – his voice rising and falling in a Shakespearean vibrato. Mrs Micawber, sitting upright in an easy chair, gazed at him proudly. Thomas and Amelia Begs, sat next to each other on the *chaise-longue* and Mrs Begs glanced apprehensively at her husband, noticing his eyelids becoming heavier as he struggled to concentrate. Emma and Ridger sat next to each other on dining chairs, and she watched her fiancé from the corner of her eye as he struggled to learn a speech from a piece of paper clutched tightly in his lap. Young Wilkins was sunk into another easy chair, watching his father with the detached eye of a critic. The twins sat on the floor at their mother's feet, looking up at their father with wide-eyed amazement, enthralled by his delivery, but confused by its content.

'"This sleep is sound indeed",' Micawber said, raising his voice several decibels.

Mr Begs's eyes blinked, and his attention swam into focus once more.

'"This is a sleep",' Micawber went on, with a rainbow-curving sweep of his right hand, '"that from this golden rigol hath divorc'd so many English kings".'

Ridger, who happened to look up from his paper, caught the word *rigol*, and wondered what the devil it meant.

'"Thy due from me is tears and heavy sorrows of the blood, which nature, love and filial tenderness shall, O dear Father, pay the plenteously".'

Young Wilkins stared at his father with fascination, wondering why he had neglected to look heavenwards during the speech. That was what he, Young Wilkins would have done, he decided, now that he had become an expert in dramatics.

Micawber reached out, and mimed holding a crown. '"My due from thee is this imperial crown. Which, as immediate from thy place and blood, derives itself to me. Lo, here it sits..."'

A moment of suspense as Micawber raised the imaginary crown above his head and began to lower it. Even Young Wilkins had to admire the way his father raised his audience's expectations. Unfortunately, the moment was ruined by Agnes's entrance with a tray of sherry. Oblivious to her employer's grand performance, she approached Mrs Begs.

"Ere we are, ma'am – get that down yuh.'

Mrs Begs looked uncomfortable but accepted the sherry, while Micawber raised his voice to a stentorian level.

'"Which God shall guard: and put the world's whole strength into one giant arm. It shall not force this lineal honour from me..."'

Agnes shuffled from person to person, distributing the sherry, as Micawber struggled to concentrate on the climax of his speech.

'"This from thee, will I to mine leave, as 'tis left to me".'

Because of Agnes's intrusion, no one seemed certain whether the speech had reached its conclusion. Mrs Begs, seeing the look of disappointment and bewilderment on Micawber's face, was the first to realize the performance had ended. She clapped enthusiastically, and soon the others joined in.

'Bravo, Mr Micawber!' she said. 'I think Mr Shakespeare sleeps secure in the knowledge that he is in such gifted hands.' She turned to her husband. 'Wouldn't you agree, dear?'

Thomas Begs gave a slightly embarrassed cough. 'Oh – er – yes, yes –absolutely. Fine performance.'

Micawber beamed. 'Such excellent company is an inspiration to a player. And now, it is with unfettered pleasure….'

Agnes handed him the last glass of sherry, saying, 'Has everyone got a drink?'

Micawber grabbed the glass and glared at her.

'You have attended to our needs, thank you, Agnes,' Mrs Micawber said. Genteel but frosty.

Micawber started to speak, 'I –er – I should like to welcome words of originality from one who is an offspring – in short, our son, Wilkins Micawber, Junior.'

The parlour door slammed as Agnes exited. A momentary frown of annoyance, and then Micawber recovered rapidly as he gestured towards Young Wilkins with an encouraging smile.

Young Wilkins swapped places with his father, while Ridger's hand trembled as he studied the words of his speech.

'Regrettably,' Young Wilkins began, 'I am unqualified to rise to this splendid occasion as an orator; but, with your permission, I hope I shall acquit myself by singing you a comic song.'

Modest laughter rippled around the room, indicating a degree of relief after the recent cultural offering.

With a slight glance and a knowing smile in Ridger's direction, Young Wilkins continued, 'However, the song is by way of cele-bration, and so it is only fitting that first we reveal one of the reasons for our gathering here today.'

Ridger rose awkwardly and cleared his throat. But Young Wilkins had other plans and, like his father, took pleasure in milking every last drop of anticipation from the event before actually getting to the point.

'But!' he exclaimed, raising an index finger.

Ridger froze, and his slack-jawed look of bewilderment was noticeably juvenile, causing his mother to ponder about his future prospects.

'But!' Young Wilkins repeated dramatically. 'Before I call upon Master Ridger Begs to speak, I should like to keep you all in suspense a moment longer by calling upon my dear sister Emma to play for you.'

He smiled at his sister and gestured to the piano. Emma crossed the room with mixed feelings of pleasure and embarrassment, while Mrs Micawber led a ripple of encouraging applause. Easing herself on to the piano stool, with her hands poised over the keys, savouring the drama of silent anticipation, a trait which seemed to run in the Micawber family, Emma prepared to play.

There came a sudden pounding on the front door, which was disturbing in its insistence. Mr Begs, fully awake now, raised an enquiring eyebrow at his host. Micawber returned the look by extending his palms upwards, indicating that he had no prior knowledge of any visit.

They all listened as they heard Agnes scurrying along the hall to answer the door.

Beads of sweat shone on Micawber's bald dome as he coughed loudly and gestured towards the piano, hoping that whatever it was that had come to disturb this important soirée would soon disappear.

'Please, My Treasure, be so good as to continue with the recital.'

As Emma began the opening bars of *Für Elise*, they heard a shout from Agnes and a kerfuffle from the hallway. Suddenly the living-room door was flung open and in strode Pellinore Crestfall, followed by two of the biggest bruisers Micawber had ever set eyes on. Emma stopped playing and Micawber leapt to his feet.

'What is the meaning of this intrusion?'

Angrily, Crestfall shook his finger at Micawber. 'I have given you fair warning, Micawber. Now my patience is exhausted.' He turned to the bruisers. 'Get the piano.' He gave Emma a polite bow and lowered his voice. 'Excuse us, miss.'

Emma stood up, clearly at a loss as she looked left and right, seeing nothing as her eyes swam with tears. 'It's ruined,' she cried. 'All ruined.'

She ran from the room.

'Emma!' Ridger called after her, plaintively.

Before fainting back in her chair and clutching her bosom, Mrs Micawber managed to utter, 'Wilkins! Do something. Do something.'

Mrs Begs, concerned for her host's welfare, appealed to Young Wilkins. 'Smelling salts! Quickly!'

Unmoved, Crestfall nodded towards the sideboard and said, 'Second drawer down.'

As the bailiffs went, one to either end of the piano, Micawber lamented to the ceiling, '"The God of day has departed and we are plunged once more into darkness!"'

Amongst the chaos, it crossed Young Wilkins's mind that this was the upward-seeking supplication to the heavens his father should have employed as Prince Hal.

Ridger, at a loss during finer points of social graces and speech-making, now realized he could show some fine mettle and perhaps save the day.

'Don't touch that piano!' he warned the bailiffs.

Due to their formidable appearance, the bailiffs were unused to being spoken to in this way, and exchanged malicious grins as they anticipated the thrill of combat. One of them cracked his knuckles.

Crestfall put out a placatory hand towards Ridger. 'I wouldn't, sir, if I were you. They don't abide by any rules of conflict.'

Hesitating, but without taking his eyes off the knuckle-cracking bailiff, Ridger addressed Young Wilkins. 'Are you with me, Master Micawber?'

To show willing, Young Wilkins moved a nervous half-pace forward. 'Well ... I ...'

'Ridger!' Mrs Begs cried. 'Please don't interfere.'

'Get that piano out,' Crestfall instructed his men.

Mr Begs, who had so far watched the scene with aloof detachment, as if he was trying to work something out, suddenly leapt to his feet. His voice was calm and rational. 'Hold your horses, Mr Crestfall. *I* will pay at least half the cost of the piano.'

Stillness fell upon the scene. Everyone stared with surprise at Mr Begs, waiting for some sort of amplification of his offer.

'As these are special circumstances,' he explained, 'and we are gathered here to celebrate the betrothal of the happy couple—'

'But I haven't announced our engagement yet, Father,' Ridger said.

'Then you had better fetch your loved one immediately.'

With puppy-dog love in his eyes, Ridger grinned at his father before hurrying out of the room. The bailiffs exchanged glances, feeling cheated now they no longer had a dispute leading to the possibility of a very bloody fight to look forward to. Mrs Micawber sat up, having made a rapid recovery, and Mr Micawber once again cast his eyes heavenwards.

'I rejoice to find that the sun has risen once more!'

'You will send me your account in due course, Mr Crestfall,' Mr Begs said.

'Very good, sir. There is just the matter of extra payment for these gentlemen.'

Crestfall waved a hand in the bailiffs' direction.

'Yes, yes!' Begs said, giving Crestfall a dismissive brushing gesture. 'And now I think that settles the matter.'

Crestfall nodded to the rest of the company. 'I'm sorry to have troubled you all.' He gave Micawber a sheepish grin. 'Er – congratulations to the happy couple.'

Disappointed at the turn of events, the bailiffs had already left the room, and Crestfall followed them out. Mrs Begs looked up at her husband admiringly and managed to catch his eye.

'Thank you, Thomas.'

Begs shook his head, as if he couldn't quite believe what had just happened, and the part he had played in this fiasco. He tapped Micawber's arm.

'If I might have a brief word in private, Mr Micawber.'

He led the way to the hallway and turned to face Micawber with a serious expression, as if what had just happened had cost him far more than money.

'This is positively the last time I will bail you out of your difficulties, Mr Micawber. Is that understood?'

Micawber nodded gravely. 'I am deeply possessed of your sensibilities, Mr Begs. And allow me to impress upon you the probability of something turning up very shortly.'

It was after he had said this that Micawber noticed a slight glint in his landlord's eye.

'That probability,' Begs said, '*could* be a certainty if it's racing in the three o'clock tomorrow.'

He returned to the living room, leaving Micawber to ponder about a flutter in tomorrow's race.

16

Rivals

ALTHOUGH HORSE RACING had become one of the most important events in the city of Melbourne, the racecourse was still
in its infancy, and the stands resembled a small cricket pavilion
and an enclosure on an English country green, albeit slightly
more dusty and brown than the lush green of the mother country.

Anyone who hadn't any religious objection to gambling and
horse racing, which was the majority of the population of
Melbourne, attended the event with a rowdy and infectious
excitement, which grew in proportion to every race, so that by
the time it neared the main race at three o'clock, the crowd had
reached a fever pitch and clamoured to find a good position by
the rails.

Emma and Mrs Begs sat together in the stands, which were
raised to a height of no more than six feet, but gave them a
reasonable view of the finishing post and most of the course. Both
had parasols, brightly coloured with tasselled fringes, and Emma
twirled hers in a jaunty fashion, while keeping an eye out for
Ridger, with whom she was now officially engaged to be married,
and every so often her eyes were drawn to the ring that sparkled
on her finger.

Mrs Begs caught her surreptitiously looking at it once more,
and smiled tolerantly, remembering her own engagement and
how happy she had been all those years ago, in spite of their
having to struggle and make sacrifices.

Squeezed tightly into the crowd of spectators, Young Wilkins stood shoulder-to-shoulder with Godfrey, waiting with mounting excitement for the horses to leave the paddock.

'Wilkins, my dear chap,' Godfrey shouted over the noise of the crowd, 'I know you don't have much money, but I hope you managed to raise enough to place a bet on Chatham Boy.'

Young Wilkins shook his head emphatically. 'I didn't.'

'But it's a racing certainty and a good price. Couldn't you have sold or pawned something in order to raise the necessary?'

Cupping a hand close to his mouth, Young Wilkins leaned closer to his friend and said, 'I've had a small wager, Godfrey, but not on Chatham Boy. I put my money on Captain Shelbourne's horse.'

Godfrey stared at his friend in astonishment as he waited for an explanation.

'I know you think me disloyal, after what Mr Begs has done, but I'm a pragmatist, Godfrey. Captain Shelbourne's horse happens to be the favourite, and it won't make any difference to Mr Begs if I choose to place my bet on Golden Pride.'

'But, Wilkins, you foolish boy,' Godfrey laughed, 'Chatham Boy's going to win.'

Young Wilkins looked smugly confident. 'I don't think so. In fact, I *know* so. Golden Pride will romp clear of Chatham Boy by at least six lengths.'

'How can you be so certain?'

'I've studied their form, and logic informs me that Golden Pride must win.'

There was an expectant rise in the noise of the crowd as the first horses began to leave the paddock, and Godfrey and Young Wilkins broke off their conversation as they both craned their necks and strained to catch a glimpse of the horses as they came towards the start.

At the paddock, Mr Begs stared at Chatham Boy with anxious pride, hardly daring to countenance defeat. He had to win! He just had to! This was more than just a horse race. Across the other side of the paddock, he caught sight of Captain Shelbourne and their eyes met briefly.

The captain was now in his sixties, an upright figure, tall and bony, with barely an ounce of fat on his frame, and a long thin, once handsome face, but now heavily lined and with sunken eyes. He still had a good head of hair, which was bleached white by the sun.

Mr Begs realized he was scowling aggressively and looked away, staring at his rival's horse instead. At his side stood Ridger, aware that something had occurred between his father and Captain Shelbourne, something more than sporting rivalry. He sensed with growing concern that winning this race was of profound importance to his father, and it had something to do with his rival. But what if his father should lose? It was still only a horse race. But he felt there was something more behind it.

'Listen, Father,' Ridger began reassuringly, 'Chatham Boy's a great horse, but if he should come second ...'

Begs snorted angrily. 'I don't care if he comes second; as long as Shelbourne's horse comes third. Come on, let us go to the finishing post and see the race.'

He marched off, weaving in and out of the spectators. Ridger followed closely behind, his head jumbled with confusion as he tried to work out what his father had just told him.

17

Mr Micawber's Moral Dilemma

A s Mrs Micawber sat on the *chaise-longue* in the parlour, calmly sipping tea, Mr Micawber paced restlessly back and forth. He gave his pocket watch a cursory glance.

'It is a moral dilemma,' he announced. 'Should I adhere to my own precepts, avoid ambiguity and, in short, refrain from gambling? Or should I indulge the caprices of fate and, in short, risk it?'

Mrs Micawber's cup went down with a positive clink.

'I have always said, have I not, Wilkins, that what is best suited to your peculiar temperament is, I am convinced, a certainty.'

Not hearing what he wished to hear, with great disappointment and a deep sigh, Micawber slumped into a chair. 'You are right, My Dearest. I am always willing to defer to your good sense.'

'No, hear me out, Wilkins. Mr Begs has assured you that his horse is a certainty. Therefore, it is not so much a fling with fate as a golden opportunity and a chance to invest in our future.'

It took a moment to register what his wife had said, but as soon as it had sunk in, Micawber leapt to his feet, beaming happily.

'Never was a man blessed with a sensible union such as ours.'

He took out his pocket watch and checked the time. Staring closely at it, a frown wrinkling his brow, he produced a small exclamation of concern. 'Hmm?' He frantically tapped the watch face.

Agnes came in to take away the remains of the tea things.

'Agnes, what time is it?' Micawber asked.

Agnes shrugged. 'I dunno, I'm sure.'

Micawber clicked his tongue impatiently. 'You must have some idea. I make it two o' clock.'

Agnes laughed shrilly, which always irritated her mistress.

'Oh, no! It's past three. That much I do know. 'Cause that's the time Tim O'Sullivan leaves for Geelong – and he's as regular as a clock.'

Agnes watched her employer with interest as he stared at his watch, his eyes bulging and desperate.

'It's stopped,' he said.

Tension mounted as the starter raised his flag, but Thomas Begs seemed distant and distracted now that the race was almost underway. As the starter brought the flag down, a sudden roar went up from the crowd, and the horses surged forward, their hoofs beating out a frantic rhythm on the harsh, sun-parched ground.

A sharp stab of disappointment penetrated Ridger as he saw his father's horse get off to a poor start. The horses thundered past where he and his father stood at the rails. They galloped flat out on the first circuit, but Chatham Boy had made little ground and was one of the back markers, while Captain Shelbourne's horse was at the front of the pack and soon took second place as it began to challenge the leader. As the horses hurtled towards the first bend, out of sight of where they stood, Ridger noticed his father staring at him, as if he couldn't bear to see his horse losing.

'What's wrong? Can't you bear to look?'

Begs stared at his son like a penitent seeking absolution, and he spoke hurriedly. 'There's something I have to tell you, Ridger. I should have told you a long time ago but—'

The spectators roared with excitement as Captain Shelbourne's horse took the lead by a neck. Ridger ignored his father and stood on tiptoe as he tried to glimpse Chatham Boy's position.

'He's still last. He's the back marker.'

The urgency increased in Begs's voice as he struggled to regain his son's attention.

'Listen to me, Ridger: you'll be married soon, with children of your own. You have to know your own history.' He placed a hand on Ridger's arm. 'And you must face up to it – without a sense of shame.'

Ridger, suddenly alert to his father's need to speak of something deeply troubling, turned his attention away from the race. His father spoke quickly, as if he wanted to tell his story before the race ended.

'I did not emigrate from England as you have been led to believe: I was transported.'

Ridger's mouth fell open, and he looked around to see if anyone close by had overheard his father's confession. But everyone was intent on watching the race, which would soon draw to a close as the horses thundered along just two furlongs from home.

'I was twelve when my mother died,' Begs continued hurriedly. 'There was no one to whom I could turn. I was cold and hungry. I stole a loaf of bread and some bacon. I was caught and sentenced to seven years' transportation. The voyage was a vision of hell. Twelve years old and I was a convict and a thief. I stole again … on the ship. Someone informed and I was brought before the captain. I could have received a hundred lashes, but he took pity on me and clapped me in irons for the rest of the voyage. It was a living death. The stench and the lice and – there was not a minute passed on that voyage that I did not curse that captain's pity.'

Ridger frowned deeply, and stared into his father's eyes with genuine concern. 'You were a convict. Why have you never told me this?'

His father shrugged, unable to answer. Ridger was suddenly pushed, and he felt an elbow digging into the small of his back as a spectator attempted to view the last moments of the race. Ridger and his father were jostled by the excited crowd, and a surge in excitement, mingled with cries of disappointment, rose to a crescendo as the leading horses neared the finishing post. Now that Begs had unburdened himself of his shameful history, he stretched himself to his full height and focused his attention on the colours of the leading jockeys.

'Chatham Boy's one of the leaders,' Ridger yelled. 'He can do it! He can do it!'

Begs smiled confidently and, whatever the outcome of the race, he knew he was a winner now.

Ridger, his fists waving above his head, screamed himself hoarse. 'Yes! Yes! He's got the edge. Go on Chatham Boy. Go on! You can do it!'

In the stands, Emma Micawber was on her feet, cheering her future father-in-law's horse. As Chatham Boy passed the winning post half a length ahead of Golden Pride, Emma shrieked louder than any other ladies in the stands. And, as the horses slowed their pace, now that the race was over, she suddenly became aware of her social blunder and looked round with embarrassment. No other ladies had risen from their seats. She sat down quickly and glanced towards Mrs Begs, expecting to see an expression of disapproval. But her future mother-in-law giggled and patted her hand reassuringly.

As Agnes exited, the door banged shut, sounding to Micawber like a coffin lid closing. He shivered and continued to stare agonizingly at his pocket watch. Anger animated him, as he blamed the heavens:

'The God of day has sunk without trace! Our hopes eclipsed! Our prospects dashed! We are forever floored.'

Mrs Micawber sighed deeply. 'Alas! We have been repaid for a wrong, Wilkins. If we had kept possession of My Dear Mama's clock ...'

Far from dissipating his anger, Micawber saw where her argument was leading, and explained in an extremely aggravated tone, 'We should be in exactly the same straits, for, if you remember, that instrument had ceased to function.'

Mrs Micawber gave her husband the sort of smile she reserved for the twins when she was attempting to explain why they shouldn't do something of which she disapproved.

'Allow me to diverge from your opinion for a moment, My Love. I have always believed in your integrity – you know that. But when you accepted money for My Dear Mama's clock, knowing it to be faulty, it was an uncharacteristic malpractice. Of course, I realize you were pushed to the limits, but I have always been of the opinion that one bad turn is paid by another.'

There was a long pause while Micawber thought about this, inwardly struggling with doubts that bounced back and forth between logic and superstition. Eventually, he came down in favour of the latter, and smiled beatifically, as if he now possessed some universal truth.

'As usual, My Dear, you have hit the nail squarely upon the head! I am a knave and a swindler. I, who have never committed a dishonest act in my life, have cheated a pawnbroker. He may charge excessive rates of interest, and some may call him usurer, but he was honest.'

Mrs Micawber watched a sudden thought flitting through her husband's head before he bounded from the room.

'Wilkins!' she called, as she rose from the *chaise-longue.* 'Where are you going?'

Having already collected his hat and cane from the hall, Micawber popped his head round the door. 'There is a universal gravity of right and wrong and I have fallen from grace. I must make amends, or chance will continue to frown upon us and erode our fortunes.'

His suddenly bright and moon-like face disappeared from view. Presently Mrs Micawber heard the front door slam. She turned and looked at the empty space on the mantelpiece, on which had stood the carriage clock of her Dear Mama, and she smiled triumphantly.

Now that the race was over, the spectators drew away from the rails, pushing and elbowing their way towards much needed refreshments. Young Wilkins remained clutching the rails, his knuckles white with tension. He didn't even notice the over-weight man who barged into him, but clung tight to the rail, his eyes fixed on the track, wishfully imagining a different outcome as he saw the ghost of Captain Shelbourne's horse overtaking Chatham Boy.

'I am stunned,' he said, in a croaking whisper.

Godfrey leaned close to him. 'What was that?'

'What I have just witnessed is beyond my comprehension.'

Godfrey slid an arm across Young Wilkins's shoulders. 'But, Wilkins, you read your father's article about Thomas Begs's horses, and Chatham Boy in particular. You were handed infor-mation on a silver platter. Far be it for me to preach, but you should have followed parental advice on this occasion.'

'I know, but when one's parents have a predisposition for, shall we say, gilding the proverbial lily, what is one supposed to do? And, dash it all, Chatham Boy was nowhere near the leaders until two furlongs from the finish.'

Godfrey laughed heartily. 'I think that's tactical racing, my dear chap.'

'Even so,' Young Wilkins muttered gloomily.

'Cheer up, Wilkins. At least one of us heeded your father's jour-nalistic prediction, and I have won enough for us both to worship at the temple of Bacchus.'

Chuckling joyfully, Godfrey pulled his friend away from the rails, and they weaved through the noisy throng towards a crowded marquee.

Thomas Begs and his son, excited and elated, their feelings

bubbling but kept within the bounds of decorum, hastened past the stands to see their horse and to congratulate their jockey. Begs looked up to see his wife and Emma Micawber smiling and applauding, and he acknowledged them with a smile and a wave. Ridger grinned at Emma and his eyes suddenly filled with tears of happiness. He felt overwhelmed by her beauty and what had been a truly remarkable day.

They approached Chatham Boy as the jockey was dismounting. The horse gleamed with soapy sweat and steam rose from its flanks.

'Well done, Declan,' Begs congratulated his jockey. 'You rode a breathtaking race.'

'Sure, I couldn't go wrong with a horse like Chatham Boy,' the jockey replied modestly, but clearly elated by his win.

Begs slapped him on the back and walked to the front of Chatham Boy. As he stroked the horse's blaze, his attention focused on Golden Pride, who was surrounded by a stunned crowd of followers, none of whom had expected their favourite to come second. Unintentionally, Begs caught Captain Shelbourne's eye, and they held each other's look for a moment.

Suddenly, Captain Shelbourne strode towards Begs, and his family watched the confrontation with interest.

'Congratulations!' he said. 'He's a fine horse. You have trained him well.'

Begs, tense and uncomfortable, accepted the compliment with a nod and half smile. 'Thank you,' he said stiffly.

As if to save Begs further embarrassment, Shelbourne turned on his heels and walked away. Begs moved after him quickly and grabbed his arm. Shelbourne turned back, gaping at Begs with a look of astonishment, and frowning hard because of the audacity of the physical contact.

'I would also like to thank you,' Begs said hurriedly, 'for keeping my secret all these years. It was extremely honourable of you, and I appreciate it.'

Shelbourne smiled and held out his hand. 'No sense in opening old wounds.'

Once they had shaken hands, Begs watched Shelbourne return to his party, and felt grateful and at ease with himself now that some ghosts had been put to rest. Ridger, who had been watching his father carefully, edged up beside him.

'Was that him? The captain of the transport ship?'

Begs, who hadn't credited his son with much sensitivity before, seemed surprised by his insightfulness. 'How did you know?'

Ridger smiled warmly. 'I'm just beginning to learn things about my father that I never knew before.'

As Begs held his son's stare, he was amazed at how their relationship had improved in such a short space of time, and there was now a more mature and mutual understanding between them.

'Come,' he said, 'I think it's time we celebrated our win.'

18

Full Circle

THE PAWNBROKER WAS polishing a silver trophy when the shop bell tinkled. He looked up, and his expression was that of a heavyweight pugilist floored by a lightweight novice as he caught sight of Micawber strutting through the door. His mouth fell open, giving him a deeply gormless expression, and he was clearly finding it confusing to grasp the sheer audacity of this visitation.

Micawber approached the counter and produced the pawn ticket with a flourish. 'I am here to redeem that precious scientific instrument, made for the benefit of mankind's linear and chronological progression within the universe. In short – one clock!'

Deeply suspicious of Micawber, and hardly daring to take his eyes off him, the open-mouthed ogre shuffled backwards and attempted to search for the carriage clock. He had to take his eyes off Micawber for a moment, in order to check the item against the number on the pawn ticket, and when he looked back, he seemed almost surprised that Micawber was still there. Not only that, but the customer was smiling helpfully. This was too much for the pawnbroker, who promised himself he would shut early and spend a few hours in the grog shop getting slowly inebriated.

'That'll be one pound and five shillings,' he said, pushing the clock across the counter towards Micawber.

Micawber stood back in alarm. 'Five shillings' interest!'

An objection to the interest he charged was something the

pawnbroker understood and was used to dealing with, and his expression told Micawber it was time to settle his dues.

'Yes – well – ahem! An inconsiderable sum when one considers the extraordinary and edifying truth that it has been my good fortune to acquire.'

He gave the pawnbroker the money, picked up the clock and started for the door.

'I never thought I'd clap eyes on you again,' the pawnbroker said.

Micawber opened the door and the bell tinkled. He turned to address the pawnbroker before making his exit.

'You behold a poorer but wiser man. I have thrown myself upon the mercy of fate, and she is now in receipt of her premium, which means I am covered and protected, and can step out into the mortal world – confident that something is bound to turn up.'

The pawnbroker was still none the wiser about what had just happened. The last thing Micawber heard before closing the door was a puzzled grunt, not unlike the sound of a dog in a disturbed sleep.

As Micawber strolled along Collins Street, a young child with her mother caught his infectious smile and returned it. Micawber doffed his hat to both mother and child and continued on his way, reflecting on how fortunate he was to be alive on such a glorious day. And he just knew, beyond all doubt, that something was bound to turn up.

PART TWO

19

The Rule of Three

IT WAS LESS than four weeks until Christmas Day and still the
Micawber family saw no end to their financial plight. In recent
months, since Emma Micawber's betrothal to Ridger Begs, her
father had another article published in the *Melbourne Chronicle*,
but the money barely provided sufficient funds for more than the
basic requirements, and he also paid to have the carriage clock
repaired, which he considered necessary in case they were forced
to pawn it once more. And now Mr Begs's offer of free rent for a
month had long since run out and debts were mounting once
more, including the outstanding sum for the upright piano. A visit
from an irate Pellinore Crestfall was expected at any time, for not
a single penny had been paid since their landlord's intervention
when he had contributed half of the debt.

They dreaded the creditors' forceful knock on the door, which
sent them scurrying silently into hiding, pretending that no one
was at home, secure in the knowledge that Agnes could no longer
inadvertently provide ingress to an insistent creditor, because
their housekeeper had departed over a month ago. Weary of
never receiving any wages, tired of excuses, and exhausted by the
constant frustrations of attempting to survive on next to nothing,
she had departed for pastures new, and found employment
working for a family where the man of the house had a thriving
business as one of Melbourne's finest butchers, and who was also
engaged as a barrister on occasions.

But the knock they no longer feared was that of Mr Larkfield, because now Micawber could capitalize on his landlord's son being welcomed into the bosom of his family. Surely no landlord would badger a tenant over a trifling sum of money when his own son would soon be married to the tenant's daughter. As far as Micawber was concerned rent arrears was the least of their problems, and he was now supremely confident that the position he had been waiting for had at last turned up. He had applied for employment as a shipping clerk at a tea and coffee importing company, and the job interview was barely a week away. So, in order that their landlord remained tractable, he made certain Emma told her fiancé about his job prospects, hoping word would get back to his prospective son-in-law's father.

But Micawber was aware that even if he were fortunate enough to fill the vacancy as shipping clerk, the employment was not due to start until the New Year, just over four weeks away, and a family could starve to death in that time! Apart from which, it would mean a Christmas of utter destitution and despair. It would not be the first such Yuletide spent in penury, not by a long shot, but they had made this trip to the other side of the world in order to put the past behind them and begin life afresh, positive that success was within their grasp. But the last two articles he had written and submitted to Mr Kynoch had been rejected, though Micawber was not without hope, and he had spent the morning writing his third article that week. Somehow he felt a surge of optimism, aware that there might be some truth in the age-old superstition of fortune arriving at the third attempt, and had rushed off to the newspaper office to see if he could tempt the editor with his offering, an article about festive ales and punches, which he hoped would inspire feelings of nostalgia, for Christmases with snow and jolly log fires and merry-making drinks.

While he was away pestering Mr Kynoch, Mrs Micawber sat in the parlour, squeezed into the corner of the *chaise-longue*, and was deep in conversation with her daughter, the discussion being solely about Emma's rosy future with a young man whose father was a wealthy landowner. Mrs Micawber's hands were all aquiver as she nervously excused her family's lack of monetary support.

'My Dear Emma!' she trilled. 'If only your papa had found an intellectual occupation, as befits a man of his talents, we might have been in a position to keep our heads elevated and offer a dowry, however insignificant the sum. However, unless some breathtaking changes in fortune occur, it looks as if a dowry might not be within the realms of the attainable.'

Emma gave her mother an understanding smile. 'I have already spoken with Mrs Begs and she intimated that a dowry is not expected.'

'Oh, did she? And what did she mean by that?'

'She meant no harm, Mama. She was being – I think she was being understandably modern.'

Mrs Micawber frowned deeply. 'Modern?'

'This is a new world, and we are witnessing many changes, Mama. Just this year they have that telegraph that everyone's talking about, and they can send messages instantly to Williamstown.'

Mrs Micawber waved a dismissive hand. 'I really cannot see the point. Why would one pay sixpence to send a scant message a distance of eleven miles?'

'I expect it is for urgent messages,' Emma suggested, a trifle weakly; but at least she felt pleased at having deflected the conversation from her lack of a dowry.

'Goodness gracious! Whatever next?' her mother said, shaking her head. 'Soon the art of letter writing will have vanished.'

They heard a positive knock on the front door and froze, their eyes locked together in trepidation, fearing that unannounced visitors could mean rampaging creditors. As they listened for Agnes's footsteps, forgetting she had left their employment, there came another insistent knock. Emma's eyes flitted to the piano, praying that it was not Mr Crestfall, as her musical abilities were progressing in leaps and bounds.

They remained silent and tense, huddled together on the *chaise-longue*. As it was blisteringly hot, the living room window was wide open, although a view into the room was masked by lace curtains. Suddenly, they were startled by a voice from the veranda outside.

'Is anyone home? It's only me – Godfrey McNeil.'

Emma felt her mother's grip on her hand relax.

'I hope it's not inconvenient,' Godfrey persisted. 'It's just a courtesy call.'

'You'd better show him in,' Mrs Micawber whispered urgently, as if she had forgotten their caller was not a creditor.

Emma rose hurriedly, and called out, 'I'll be with you in a moment, Mr McNeil.'

She went out into the hall, opened the front door, and found herself looking up into Godfrey's smiling face, and it flitted through her head that here was a man who was nowhere near as handsome as her betrothed, but his personality more than made up for his physical shortcomings, although he wasn't exactly unattractive.

She banished the intruding thoughts from her mind, and noticed he was clutching a cloth bag, held close to his chest as if it contained a precious, fragile object.

'I hope I'm not calling at an inopportune moment, Miss Micawber.'

'Not at all, Mr McNeil. Although I must leave shortly to fetch the twins from their scholastic endeavours. But please come in and reacquaint yourself with my mother.'

She led the way into the living room and closed the door.

Mrs Micawber smiled politely. 'To what do we owe this pleasure, Mr McNeil?'

'The last time I was here, after I had the good fortune to

become acquainted with your son, I couldn't help but notice your family's fondness for port wine. I hope you won't think this presumptuous of me, but I also noticed that the drink was poured directly from the bottle.'

Seeing Mrs Micawber's puzzled frown was in danger of becoming a scowl, McNeil continued hurriedly, 'Not that I have ever decanted a bottle myself – it is always direct from bottle to glass for me. But in a welcoming family such as yours, I thought it fitting to own an elegant decanter. Please excuse the coarse covering.'

With a conjuror's flourish, McNeil flicked the sacking cover from the object he was holding to reveal a crystal decanter, and handed it to Mrs Micawber. 'It's just a small token, ma'am, for your kindness in welcoming me to the bosom of your family a while back.'

Mrs Micawber's eyes widened with delight. 'Why, Mr McNeil! Such a splendid gift. The crystal is beautiful, and this etching of fleurs-de-lis is most distinctive.'

Godfrey McNeil threw a shy grin in Emma's direction, and their eyes met. All at once, he felt a melting sensation and a pounding in his breast. She too felt a sudden glow, and began to blush.

'Thank you, Mr McNeil,' Mrs Micawber said. 'This is really more than generous. Please do be seated and spend a little time with us.'

Godfrey McNeil glanced at Emma's mother briefly, but he found it hard to steer his gaze away from the daughter. He crossed the room and sat on a dining chair.

Mrs Micawber stared at her visitor wistfully, wishing he was financially well placed. Not that she had anything against young Begs as such, but his grasp of the finer nuances of the English language was sadly lacking. Whereas young McNeil filled one with confidence, and gave one a reassurance that things in this modern world were not necessarily changing for the worse.

She smiled at her guest and fluttered her eyelids. 'My son tells me you have been instructing him in the art of dramatic recitation.'

Godfrey looked suitably unassuming, but cast a warm glance towards Emma.

'I have merely offered him a little encouragement, ma'am.'

'I fear you are being modest, Mr McNeil. Since you took him under your wing, we have all seen a great improvement in his recitations.'

'A great improvement!' Emma reiterated. 'But please tell us where you gained this talent for directing drama. Surely you must have had experience as an actor yourself.'

'I have no experience as an actor,' Godfrey answered. 'I've never been on a stage in my life.'

He gazed into Emma's eyes and could see her forming another question, so changed the subject quickly. 'And where is your father today?'

'He has gone to see the editor at the *Melbourne Chronicle*.'

'Ah! All being well, there will soon be other interesting articles for us to read.'

Emma looked uncertain about the prospects and smiled weakly. 'He has written an essay in praise of Yuletide ales and punches.'

'Alas!' Mrs Micawber exclaimed. 'Two of his writings, submitted in under a week, have fallen on hard times. When there is so much news to report, so much crime on the streets, and extra ships being used for prisons....'

Mrs Micawber broke off with a despairing gesture.

Godfrey smiled encouragingly. 'But your husband has persevered. He knows what it means to try, try and try again. His third attempt may prove to be the successful one.'

'I hope you are accurate in your prediction, Mr McNeil. But I thought my husband's first two efforts were impressive, so in the circumstances I can't help but feel disheartened.'

Emma squeezed her mother's hand. 'Please try not to worry, Mama. I'm sure Papa will be fortunate this time.'

Godfrey caught himself staring at Emma's hand, placed gently over her mother's, and he imagined he was the recipient of such a brush with tenderness.

Emma's eyes darted to the carriage clock on the sideboard, and she gave a sharp intake of breath and stood up. 'I really must collect the twins from their schooling.'

Godfrey rose and said, 'Please allow me to accompany you.'

Mrs Micawber's mouth tightened disapprovingly.

'Thank you,' Emma said, 'but I don't think that will be necessary. It is a distance of less than half a mile.'

Godfrey placed a hand over his heart as he gazed into her eyes. 'I realize you are betrothed to a worthy young man, and far be it for me to compromise your relationship by indecorous behaviour, but all I mean to offer you is my most sincere goodwill to assist you in a safe passage through a city that has become increasingly threatening since the influx of so many immigrants and the growth of Canvas Town.'

Godfrey sounded so sincere, and his motive so genuine, that Emma offered him a tiny smile, and even her mother nodded her approval.

'Thank you, Mr McNeil,' she said. 'I am most grateful to you for safeguarding my daughter.'

'It is my pleasure entirely, ma'am.'

Frowning, Emma turned towards the door. For months now she had convinced herself that she found her parents' long-windedness wearisome, and was equally convinced that her fiancé's unspoken devotion to her was preferable to a man given to making empty speeches. She had suppressed the true feelings of pride she felt for her parents' command of the English language and their erudition, mistakenly thinking she found it tiresome. But now it suddenly struck her how dissatisfied she was. If only Ridger was more skilled in the art of conversation. If only he could find a few simple words to express his feelings. And if only he could be a little more like Godfrey McNeil.

Not long after Emma had departed, accompanied by Godfrey, Mr Micawber bounded into the living room, beaming proudly, his chest thrust out like a strutting bird.

Mrs Micawber, who was laying the table for supper, said, 'I see by the smile on your face, Wilkins, that Mr Kynoch has come to his senses after rejecting your last two submissions.'

Micawber produced a bottle of port from behind his back and held it aloft. 'The Fates are three, the Furies three, and the fountain from which Hylas drew water was presided over by three nymphs. We humans are body, mind and spirit – three! The world is earth, sea and air – three! And nature is animal, vegetable and mineral – three! I should have realized my article which is submission number three, was bound for success. Mark my words! This rule of three is a universal truth. But why do you look at me with an expression of scepticism, My Treasure?'

'If you will allow me a minor observation, Wilkins, the examples you gave me as a universal rule of three far exceeded the quota.'

Mentally counting, Micawber looked up towards the ceiling. 'I mentioned the Fates, Furies and Nymphs—'

'Precisely!' Mrs Micawber interrupted. 'You should have stopped at example number three.'

With his free hand, Micawber silently counted the rest of his list, ending with a triumphant smile. 'And I gave another three examples, making it six. Had it been five or seven, then I would be in accordance with your objection, My Dear. But twice three is six. So, you see, the rule still applies, just as it would have done had I produced another three examples, making it a total of nine. Now all this untangling of the examples I gave has exhausted me, so I think a glass of this fine ...'

Micawber stopped as he walked to the sideboard to fetch glasses and spotted the cut-glass decanter with its stylish crest.

Momentarily tongue-tied, he gestured at the decanter, and raised enquiring eyebrows to his wife.

'A gift,' she explained. 'We had a visitor.'

Micawber's face lit up. 'Was it Mr Begs, our worthy landlord?'

'It was Godfrey McNeil.'

Although he felt initial pangs of disappointment, Micawber soon recovered. 'Splendid chap!' he said. 'But this fine ornament looks mightily extravagant. And according to Young Wilkins, his friend has not yet found employment and lives in a shack in Canvas Town. How, therefore, might he arrive bearing such a costly gift?'

Mrs Micawber shrugged. 'Perhaps it belongs to him and, as he lives alone, he has no need of it.'

'Wherever young Godfrey acquired this fine article, it is appreciated and I will use it forthwith.' He banged the bottle down on to the sideboard and fumbled excitedly in his pocket. 'But first, allow me to demonstrate another example of the rule of three.' He held up three tickets.

'I see you holding three tickets, Wilkins, but I am none the wiser unless an explanation is forthcoming.'

Micawber was like a child, feverish with excitement. 'After I had done the deal with Mr Kynoch, my perambulations took me past that fine new building, the Queen's Theatre. And if you will permit me to wallow in sentimentality for a moment, do you recall the times we spent in the mother country worshipping at the Temple of Thespis? Do you remember the hours we whiled away in London's Royal Theatre of Drury Lane, being captivated by the works of our most eminent dramatists and performers?'

Mrs Micawber's bland expression masked an inclination to reveal her true feelings on the subject of their past visits to London theatres, which had been seldom; and on one of the rare occasions they had visited the theatre at Drury Lane, their seats had been so high up, the bird's eye view of the actors was inclined to make her feel giddy.

But Micawber failed to notice her lack of enthusiasm, and

went on, 'These tickets represent a nostalgic journey to a land of intellectual achievement for a few hours of stimulation and enlightenment. In short, we are off to the theatre this evening.'

'What are we going to see? A play by Mr William Shakespeare, perhaps?'

Mr Micawber paused before continuing. 'We are privileged in seeing The Great Jupiter himself.'

'The Roman god? What is he doing in Melbourne?'

'Two shows daily. The Great Jupiter is the name he has chosen to use in his profession of magician extraordinaire.'

Mrs Micawber flashed her husband a childlike smile. 'Oh, I do so love conjuring tricks. But to return momentarily to your rule of three, is that why you purchased three tickets?'

'I suppose it might have been, inasmuch as it was coincidental, yet further proof – if any were needed – that the rule has some mysterious influence over our existence. But my conscious decision in purchasing three was so that Young Wilkins might benefit from an evening of artistic entertainment.'

'But his ambitions lie in classical drama, not leisurely amusements.'

'Nevertheless, he will observe and learn the great art of presentation.'

Mrs Micawber frowned deeply, and her eyes became distant.

'Why do you look so pensive, My Dearest?'

'I was thinking – it's a great pity that Emma cannot visit the theatre with us.'

Micawber shook his head and pulled the cork from the port bottle. 'It is indeed a great pity. But since Agnes deserted us, we cannot leave the twins alone. And I thought, as our daughter is having lavish attention heaped upon her by the Begs family, a night of domestic duty seemed small recompense for such munificent circumstances.'

'And, perhaps, Wilkins, she will be taken to the theatre by young Ridger, so she may get to see it after all.'

'I expect she will,' Micawber said with little conviction, because he guessed that his future son-in-law had little interest in the arts, even in light diversions such as magic shows.

Micawber made little humming noises of contentment as he poured two glasses of port. 'I will decant the rest of the bottle shortly,' he said.

As Mrs Micawber accepted a glass, she looked nervously at her husband and said, 'Man cannot live by bread alone, I can quite understand, Wilkins.'

'The sentiment is easy to follow, My Dearest, but the linear progression of your senses discombobulates the organ of my intellect. In short, I missed the point of your statement.'

'I mean, Wilkins, a bottle of port, while not exactly a necessity, is nonetheless vital to our wellbeing. However, purchasing theatre tickets when we are only weeks away from Christmas, and finances being still somewhat rocky, seems – if you don't mind my mentioning it – a trifle extravagant, if not foolhardy.'

'Be that as it may,' Micawber said with a flutter of the hand, 'I am utterly confident that the job as a shipping clerk is in my grasp.' He saw his wife was about to utter another objection, so continued hurriedly, 'Yes, yes, I know the post cannot be taken up until 1856, but that is a mere four weeks distant, and once the post is secured, well—' He smiled, toasted the air with his glass and took a sip. 'Mm, yes, where was I? Yes, securing remunerative employment with Tweeding and Hobson, the finest tea and coffee importers, will open doors. Open doors! In other words, credit will not be difficult to obtain.'

20

The Great Jupiter

THE QUEEN'S THEATRE was packed out for the third night of
the great illusionist's show. The magician's manager stood at
the back of the grand circle, surveying all the heads with satisfaction, knowing that the takings from the performances this
week would be enough to pay for first-class berths when they
returned to London and began a grand tour of all the major
towns and cities in Great Britain.

Checking the time on his pocket watch, he saw that at this
point in the show there was a difference of only thirty seconds
from the previous night's show. That was how the Great Jupiter
liked to run things, with a mathematical precision. Another five
minutes and the show would be over. For the sixth time that week
he smiled at what he knew was a near perfect performance; but a
discordant sound wiped the smile from his face and caused him
to wince. If only they could afford to tour their own musicians,
instead of having to hire these amateurs!

The Great Jupiter wore a long black cloak decorated with
geometric symbols in many colours. He gave the cloak a flourish
and then offered his attractive assistant a hand to step into a large
three-sided gold box. The assistant was dressed like an
Elizabethan boy, with breeches, but tighter fitting, so that her
slender legs could be admired but were still within the bounds of
decency. Her hair was blonde and curly, and she had bright red
lips and a rather large beauty spot on her left cheek. She smiled

alluringly at the audience before the magician pulled a curtain across the front of the box and turned it slowly around. When it had turned full circle, he whipped back the curtain to reveal that it was empty, and the audience gasped. And just to show that she couldn't have climbed out of a secret door at the back, he moved the wheeled box towards one side of the stage, and then the other. In any case, the box was raised at least two feet off the ground, which would have revealed the assistant's legs had she escaped from the back, and there was also no way she could have disappeared through a trapdoor in the stage.

The orchestra played brightly, soliciting hearty applause from the audience. The magician smiled and stepped forward a pace, bowed from the waist, and threw out his arms to silence the audience. He then spun the empty box once more to reveal the assistant had returned.

Smiling demurely, she took the magician's hand and stepped out of the box, as the crowd erupted with cries of 'Bravo!' and lively applause, while the tinny orchestra reached the pinnacle of their rendition, a tune which sounded as if each instrument was racing for a finishing line.

Mrs Micawber got carried away, stopped applauding, grabbed her husband's hand and squeezed it in both of hers. Mr Micawber turned to his wife and smiled his approval of the performance and her actions.

The hubbub died down, and the audience – who thought the show had ended – became suddenly aware that there was still more to come. Young Wilkins who was sitting on the other side of his mother, leant forward expectantly in his seat, wondering, like so many others, what the Great Jupiter could possibly do to better his previous illusion.

Another box, identical to the one on stage, was wheeled on, and the Great Jupiter moved both boxes so that they stood juxtaposed on opposite sides of the stage, with a gap of about fifteen feet between them. He then helped his assistant into the box on the left side of the stage, and she stood there smiling and posing while he crossed to the other empty box, pulled the curtain across, and turned it around so that it faced upstage. The orchestra played furiously, their violins screeching maniacally, as the magician returned to the first box, and after another flourish of his cloak, drew the curtain across. He spun the box so that its back was facing the audience, and walked smartly to the centre of the stage between the two boxes. The orchestra stopped playing, and the audience fell in with the expectant silence as the Great Jupiter raised his arms and spoke in a deep baritone.

'Ladies and gentlemen, I will now attempt to pass my assistant through time and space, and this unique sorcery – which has never before been attempted until I discovered this arcane method – will happen through my sheer will and determination....' His voice began to rise. 'With the aid of supernatural forces – BY JUPITER!'

He began writhing and gesturing to-and-fro between the boxes, as the orchestra's percussion began a drum roll. When it had reached its peak, he dashed to the first box, spun it round, and tore back the curtain to reveal the empty chamber, before haring across to the second box, where he spun it to face front, and whipped back the curtain to reveal his grinning assistant.

The orchestra began playing frantically again as the audience went wild, rising to their feet and applauding, shouting and whistling. The magician gestured to his assistant who posed before curtsying and bowing. She left the stage as the magician milked the audience for more applause by suddenly producing bouquets of silk flowers, appearing as if from thin air. He left the stage and returned eight times, and each time he returned he produced coloured silks and over-sized playing cards, so that the audience was left with a good lasting impression.

After he had finally departed, and it was obvious he was not about to return, the applause died to a trickle, and the orchestra played on but sounded half-hearted now the performance had ended.

As Mr Micawber, his wife and Young Wilkins shuffled out of the theatre with the rest of the audience, all chattering and theorizing on how the Great Jupiter was able to deceive them in such an agreeable fashion, a familiar figure stood in the street facing the theatre entrance, and it seemed clear to Micawber that they were heading towards a confrontation. His mood, raised by the intellectual challenge of finding the answer to the secrets of the conjuring tricks, was confounded by this collision with his landlord's rent collector, and he struggled to find an excuse for their profligacy.

There was nothing for it but to put a brave face on the situation.

'Ah! Mr Larkfield!' he said. 'I hope you enjoyed that spectacular diversion.'

'Indeed,' Larkfield agreed, though his face told another story. He was uncomfortable with the conflict but knew it was his duty to appear censorious of the Micawber family's imprudent behaviour. He glanced awkwardly at the woman at his side.

'May I introduce you to my good lady wife?'

She bobbed shyly and bade them good evening. Once they had all made the introductions, Larkfield's demeanour seemed to clash between wanting to make idle chit-chat and get down to serious business; he decided he would take a course that ran somewhere between the two.

'Yes, indeed, I enjoyed the performance, Mr Micawber, and I don't like to mix business with pleasure, but needs must when the devil drives, as the saying goes.'

Knowing Larkfield was about to bring up the indelicate subject of rent arrears, unveiling their errant conduct in a public place, Micawber grinned expansively, to include Mrs Larkfield, and said, 'This evening was a final opportunity, a slight deviation into recklessness, before your humble servant becomes a shipping clerk for that respected establishment, Tweeding and Hobson.'

Larkfield seemed both relieved and astonished. 'You are going to work for the tea and coffee people?'

'Tomorrow afternoon I have a meeting with Messrs Tweeding and Hobson, and no doubt we shall come to an amicable arrangement.'

'Well, congratulations, Mr Micawber! But I think there is something you ought to know about those men....'

At that precise moment a large, heavy-set man, with only three crooked teeth left in his mouth, barged in and lisped a message to Larkfield in a confidential manner.

'You must come at once. Our employer seeks your assistance right away.'

Mr Larkfield, whose ear was being bathed in a stream of spittle from the man, moved his head back. 'What appears to be the problem?'

The man's shifty eyes surveyed the assembled company before he leaned in again to whisper to Larkfield. Although the Micawber family couldn't hear most of what was said, they did hear the word eviction loud and clear.

Micawber felt dryness at the back of his throat and a trembling in the pit of his stomach as he thought about eviction at the hands of this bruiser.

Larkfield turned to address his wife. 'I will accompany you home post haste, my dear. Please excuse our hasty departure, Mr Micawber. Ma'am.' Larkfield acknowledged Mrs Micawber with a nod. 'We have urgent business to attend. I'll bid you all good evening.'

Micawber had been about to ask Larkfield what he had been meaning to say about Tweeding and Hobson, but he and his wife had evaporated into the crowds in an instant, and all Micawber saw was the bruiser's closely cropped head bouncing up and down through the throng. For a brief moment Micawber struggled indecisively with his thoughts, finding it difficult to make a decision of any sort. Two passers-by jostled him and he snapped out of his trance.

'Come, My Dear, we are homeward bound.'

As they walked home in silence, Mrs Micawber's mouth twitched, and she rubbed the sides of her nose hastily, a rabbit-like gesture with both hands. These were sure signs that something was deeply troubling her. But it was Young Wilkins who verbalised her concerns.

'If you don't mind my asking, Papa, have Tweeding and Hobson actually offered you employment?'

There was a pause before his father replied, 'To quote our greatest playwright, it is a "foregone conclusion".'

Young Wilkins chuckled. 'To quote an old proverb: "Do not count your chickens until they are hatched". If I'm not mistaken, your meeting at this tea importing firm tomorrow is an interview to assess your suitability for the post. Yet you led Mr Larkfield to believe that the job has already been decided upon.'

Micawber sighed loudly. 'Wilkins, Wilkins, Wilkins! Look around you. What do you see?'

As they were passing one of the less salubrious parts of Melbourne at that moment, a drunk fell out of a grog shop almost into their path.

'Well, Young Wilkins, what do you see around you?'

Young Wilkins avoided colliding with the inebriated man and said, 'A rough-looking man who was clearly intoxicated.'

'And what else?'

'Across the street a woman is screeching at her husband, and he too seems intoxicated.'

'Anything else?'

'There is a group of dirty dishevelled ragamuffins on that street corner, which makes me glad that we are not heading in that direction.'

Micawber laughed loudly, a trumpeting a note of triumph. 'You see, Young Wilkins, that is my point: how many of the ne'er-do-wells populating these streets can you envisage seated at a desk of high office, shouldering responsibility and commanding respect?'

Mrs Micawber now saw the error of her ways in doubting her husband and leapt to his defence.

'Your papa has been biding his time, hovering on the periphery of opportunity, but I now feel the time is right. This is the moment when he ascends that golden staircase to prosperity.'

Micawber slapped his chest determinedly. 'Your mama is right! All these years I have been waiting for something to turn up. And now I am looking it in the face, I am determined to rise to the challenge. I shall not shirk or fail, Young Wilkins. This was meant to be.'

But, in spite of the rallying speech, a dark cloud passed across Micawber's features.

'However, I do wish I knew what Mr Larkfield was going to inform me about my prospective employers.'

Once they arrived home, and were seated with a glass of port each, Mr and Mrs Micawber and Young Wilkins soon forgot their concerns about what Mr Larkfield had been going to say, and the conversation reverted to the eventful evening as they relived every moment of the magician's spectacular show, trying to recall each illusion or trick.

Mrs Micawber and Young Wilkins did most of the talking, while Micawber sat, his legs splayed out in front of him, and his head sunk on to his chest with an amused smile on his face.

'If only one had an opportunity to see the performance again,' Young Wilkins said. 'With the benefit of hindsight one might be able to surmise how he managed to deceive us.'

Mrs Micawber, her head tilted thoughtfully to one side, waved a finger for emphasis. 'I cannot for the life of me see how his finale was deceit. When his assistant was transferred from one box to another, surely there must have been some supernatural force at work. We could see beneath the boxes, so she could not have exited either from the back or beneath the stage. It is most perplexing.'

Mr Micawber snorted and sat up. 'Forgive me, My Dear, but the answer is simple, and I deduce there are no supernatural forces toiling to exert pressure on our powers of reasoning. In short, I know how the magician deceived us.'

Mrs Micawber didn't like the idea of there being a simple answer to the illusion; she preferred to believe there was an element of magic at work.

'But how can you, or anyone else for that matter, possibly know that?'

'By eliminating what was not possible. You have already said, My Dear, that his assistant could not have disappeared through a trapdoor because we could see under the box, and also behind it. So there is only one explanation. One of the walls inside the box was false. Once the Great Jupiter had pulled the curtain across, his assistant probably removed a false wall from a side of the box, stood at the back, and concealed herself in this compartment behind a false wall.'

'Surely if it were that simple—'

'What other explanation could there be?'

'I see what you mean, Papa,' Young Wilkins said. 'It all comes down to the presentation skills of the illusionist.'

'Exactly!' Micawber said, a tiny smile tugging the corners of his mouth.

But Mrs Micawber was not convinced by this explanation, which she found unsatisfactory, and she racked her brains to discover a flaw. She sipped her drink and thought long and hard about it. And then she realized her husband's theory had more holes than a sieve.

'In that case, tell me this, Wilkins: when his assistant stepped into the box a second time, and the other box was brought on, how do you explain how she jumped across from one side of the stage to the other box, as if by magic?'

Young Wilkins looked expectantly at his father, while he and his mother waited for the explanation. But his father was taking his time, indulging in the dramatic effect he was creating. Mrs Micawber misinterpreted this as a loophole in his theory.

'You see!' she pounced, staring at her son. 'That has well and truly stumped him.'

'Not so fast, My Angel! I do have a theory on how this extraordinary and remarkable feat was achieved. And it would indeed be truly remarkable if the answer were not so simple.'

'Come on then, Papa!' Young Wilkins urged. 'Let's hear it!'

Micawber took a sip of port and licked his lips contentedly before speaking. 'The other box, which the magician showed us was empty, in all probability used the same method of concealment – to wit: the false compartment. So that the assistant in the first box conceals herself behind the false wall, and her counterpart, who is already concealed in the false compartment in the second box, is revealed once the magician pulls the curtain open. Hey Presto! Out she steps.'

Mrs Micawber shook her head in rapid movements and her voice began to sound shrill. 'But that still doesn't explain how she managed to jump from one box to the other.'

'There were two women.'

'Two women?'

'It is the only possible explanation. The magician had two assistants, both dressed alike, with the same coiffure. Also, ingenious use of a rather prominent beauty spot on the left cheek, a deliberate ploy to fool the audience. As soon as we saw the beauty spot, we were convinced it was the same person, because our minds told us it was.'

Mrs Micawber looked crestfallen. 'Oh, but that cannot be so, Wilkins. I feel cheated now.'

Feeling concerned for his wife sensibilities, Micawber added, 'Of course, the explanation may be far more complex. My mental peregrinations into the world of wizardry are mere hypotheses, a postulation based on nothing more than my perceptions. In short, I am guessing.'

But Young Wilkins seized on the explanation with enthusiasm. 'No! Papa is right, Mama. There *must* have been two women, and unlike Edward and Emily, who are not identical twins, these assistants could well have been identical twin sisters.'

Micawber nodded. 'Another possibility.'

'Do you realize, Papa,' Young Wilkins went on, 'that you have a detective's brain? I have been reading books about the Metropolitan Police in London, and one in particular, a Detective Inspector Charley Field. He became quite celebrated because of his powers of deduction and the solving of many murder mysteries. He has long since retired from the police, but he is still in the business of detection as a private inquiry agent.'

'Yes, I think I have heard of him,' Micawber said. 'I remember reading about some of his cases in *The Times*.'

Young Wilkins rose excitedly, as he often did when he wanted to put forward an idea. 'I think, with your powers of reasoning, you might consider a career in detection. You could set yourself up as a private inquiry agent, an investigator.'

'Gracious me!' Mrs Micawber exclaimed. 'What would your papa investigate?'

'Oh, all kinds of things, Mama. People often wish to find missing relations. Or they might want stolen items traced.'

'But you mentioned this Inspector Field solved murder mysteries. I wouldn't want your father to endanger himself by associating with criminals.'

'That was when he was with the Metropolitan Police, Mama. When Mr Charley Field retired as detective inspector, his first private case was to investigate a false claimant to an inheritance, and when it was proved the claimant had no entitlement and was in fact an impostor, Field's client awarded him the sum of one hundred guineas.'

Mrs Micawber's eyes lit up as she turned to her husband. 'It would be the answer to our prayers, Wilkins.'

Micawber shook his head. 'Before we are carried away by the

lure of spectacular cases that are a civil matter, with no connection to serious felonies, let me explain about the customary assignments of these private investigators. I have read that their main business is in collecting evidence of unchaste relationships. Poking their noses through keyholes and spying on behalf of cuckolded husbands; or, conversely, seeking indelicate evidence of a husband's infidelity.'

Mrs Micawber flipped open a fan and began cooling herself rapidly. 'Goodness me! You cannot involve yourself in such scandalous behaviour, My Beloved, even for pecuniary advantage.'

'My sentiments entirely,' Micawber agreed. 'And I already have prospects with Tweeding and Hobson.'

Deflated, Young Wilkins slumped into his chair. 'It was only a suggestion.'

Micawber stood up and patted his son on the shoulder. 'And a capital suggestion it was, young sir. Should I find myself, at some future juncture, in reduced circumstances – Heaven forbid! – then I will remember your suggestion and act upon it. But for now' – he went to the sideboard and took the stopper from the decanter – 'for now I will replenish our glasses, and put my trust in a combination of Tweeding and Hobson, my mastery of administrative skills and a little bit of luck.'

As he went round and refilled the glasses, he frowned at the decanter with its fleur-de-lis symbol, and felt uncomfortable holding it. It defied explanation, why this object should arouse in him such a disagreeable feeling, but his instinct told him that this gift was like a Greek wooden horse, and the domestic bliss of his parlour could be shattered like the city of Troy.

But he kept the thought to himself.

21

Festive Ales and Punches

LESS THAN FOUR weeks until Christmas day and Melbourne suffered from oppressive heat. As he trudged along Bourke Street, avoiding pedestrians who always dashed everywhere as if their lives depended on winning a race, Micawber thought about the imminent Yuletide celebration and it suddenly struck him that the occurrence that took place in Bethlehem almost 2,000 years ago would have had not a jot of Christmas atmosphere: no mistletoe and holly, snow or jolly carol singing. And with this thought in mind, he cheered up considerably because he knew the climate in Melbourne was probably similar to that in Bethlehem all those years ago.

He stopped to mop the perspiration from his brow and someone collided with him. He was about to apologize to the fellow, but it had gone unnoticed, and was all part of the rush and tear. Micawber knew the world was changing, and lamented that it was perhaps not entirely for the better, certainly where old-world manners were concerned, although there were certain modern advantages, such as steam trains and gaslight.

Swinging his silver-topped cane, which had been polished for the occasion of his meeting with Messrs Tweeding and Hobson, he tried to put some jauntiness into his stride. He had studied his image in the bedroom mirror prior to his leaving and decided his appearance was somewhat dowdy. His top hat was showing threadbare pieces of grey in places, and he had used boot blacking to conceal the offending spaces. But with the help of his wife and daughter his appearance had been tidied and cleaned with a stitch here and there, so that no one would ever guess that he was not a man of some substance.

Tweeding and Hobson's firm was at the far end of Bourke Street, and was an imposing stone building with large rectangular windows rounded at the top in Romanesque style. A long stone veranda ran along the front of the building, and beneath its slanting roof were six ornate pillars, gilded at the top and bottom with carved leaves. To the side of the building was a driveway leading to an enormous wooden warehouse and in the driveway stood a horse and wagon, with the words 'Tweeding and Hobson, Importers of Fine Tea and Coffee, Melbourne, Victoria' in gothic lettering on the side of it.

Micawber stopped at the bottom of the steps leading up to the veranda and the open doorway and mopped his brow again. He didn't often feel this nervous, but so much of his family's future depended on this job that his usually robust manner deserted him and he began to feel sickly. But he dismissed this nervousness as a symptom of the temperature, collected himself, marched boldly up the steps and entered the company's offices.

As soon as he was inside he stopped to get his bearings, blinking several times, his eyes adjusting from bright sunshine to semi-darkness. The room in which he stood was neither an office nor a shop, but it seemed to be somewhere in between the two. There was a long counter facing him, and behind it were shelves displaying the products of the importers: colourful packets of tea and coffee, fancy tins, china teapots and coffee pots. The most dominant item was an awkward looking double pot, like two melons stuck together, and above it a notice declared boldly that this was 'The Latest in Coffee Making. The Napier Vacuum Machine for a Clear Coffee Brew.' The walls on either side of the room were decorated with framed pictures advertising the company's wares, with words of enticement on many of them.

One of them showed a dainty bone china cup filled with a dark brew, and underneath was the slogan 'Tea Is Good For You'.

But the most assertive slogan had no picture, and was framed in carved oak, with an enormous message written in gold letters against a green background. It read: 'Christ is the unseen guest at every table; the silent listener at every meal'.

Micawber stared at the message for a moment, his brows puckered in thought as he tried to imagine this invisible presence at his own meal table. He relinquished the image and walked to the counter. The room was deserted, but there was a bell on the counter with a message written on a card: 'Please ring for assistance'.

He banged the flat of his hand on the bell and it pierced the silence with its highly pitched ting. In less than half a minute, a door opened behind the counter and an elderly man, shoulders hunched, shuffled out to greet him.

'Yes?' was all he said.

'I am Mr Wilkins Micawber,' the prospective candidate boomed. 'I have come to see Messrs Tweeding and Hobson.'

The elderly man's head, which was sunk into his shoulders, twisted and focused on Micawber. 'Are they expecting you?'

'They are indeed. I have come to discuss with them the position of shipping clerk.'

'Ah!' the man exclaimed. 'You are he. You wrote the newspaper article in this week's *Chronicle*.'

Micawber beamed. 'I am that same person.'

'In that case, you'd better follow me.'

With enormous effort, his chest wheezing like a rusty wheel, the man shuffled along the counter, took a deep breath, had a fit of coughing, recovered, and raised a flap. Micawber squeezed through the gap, and the elderly man let it fall with a bang.

'Follow me,' he repeated, and led the way to the door from whence he had come.

Micawber followed him along a narrow passage, the walls

festooned with ancestral portraits. With each step he took, Micawber's jaunty confidence rose, so that by the time he reached the door through which the elderly man ushered him, his self esteem could not have risen any higher. And the reason for this was the newspaper article, published that very morning. What a blessing that was. It meant that his celebrity had gone before him, so that now he would need very little introduction. Tweeding and Hobson were already acquainted with their prospective new employee's creative talents. All he needed now was the negotiating skill to procure a lucrative salary.

The room into which Micawber had been ushered was oak panelled and lined with shelves to his right, which were full to bursting with leather-bound ledgers. On the wall to his left were framed pictures of tea clippers and sailing ships. In front of him was an enormous window, and in front of the window was a leather-topped desk, on which lay a copy of the *Melbourne Chronicle* open at the page on which his article was written. Seated behind the desk was either Mr Tweeding or Mr Hobson, and standing beside him was the other half of the partnership.

Because the sun streamed through the window, the glare put Micawber at a disadvantage, forcing him to squint at the men, who were but silhouettes outlined by the dazzling light.

'Mr Micawber!' the elderly man announced from the doorway.

'Thank you, Uncle Wilfred,' said one of the men. 'Just wait outside, this should not take long.'

Mr Micawber moved slightly to the right, with his back to the ledgers, angling himself so that he could observe his prospective employers. He saw that both men sported bushy beards.

'I'm Mr Hobson,' the man behind the desk said.

'And I'm Mr Tweeding,' said the other.

Mr Hobson's full beard was red, his bushy eyebrows were joined together in the middle, but there was very little hair upon his head, just a few wisps of ginger behind each ear. Mr Tweeding's beard was almost as bushy, but was jet black, and the skin above his lips had been shaved smooth, and he had a head of untidy shoulder-length hair. Both men were in their forties, and were formally dressed in long jackets with velvet collars and floppy bow ties, with waistcoats beneath their jackets, in spite of the stifling heat.

'Pleased to meet you, gentlemen,' Micawber said. There was a chair placed in front of the desk but he wasn't invited to sit down.

Hobson glanced up at his partner and coughed delicately before addressing Micawber. 'We very much regret that you have had a wasted journey.'

It took Micawber a moment to comprehend what Hobson had said. When he did, it was like a jolt to the heart. 'Wasted journey?' he repeated. 'But I don't understand.'

Tweeding leant over the desk and tapped Micawber's article with a querulous finger. 'This article praises liquor in all its evil forms.'

'Tweeding and Hobson do not approve of alcohol,' Hobson said. 'We are teetotal. We took the pledge many years ago and we are committed to fighting the scourge of our city streets – the demon drink.'

'I congratulate you, gentlemen,' Micawber said in a hasty attempt to recover some ground.

Tweeding and Hobson stared at one another in some confusion, and Micawber, thinking he had the advantage, pushed ahead.

'Throughout this spinning orb, from far western shores to eastern deserts, the human race is multitudinous in its pursuits, and it should be recognized that far from dividing mankind, all predilections should be tolerated, without prejudice and with regard for another person's proclivities. In short, live and let live!'

Both men regarded Micawber unblinkingly, their faces set and rigid, as if they were carved from stone.

Getting no response, and finding the silence awkward, Micawber pointed to the newspaper article with his cane and said, 'Newspapers, gentlemen, are transitory. Important enough in their immediacy in imparting the news, but once read they are cast aside like scraps of uneaten food. I guarantee, with my hand on my heart, by tomorrow my article in praise of festive ales and punches will be obliterated from people's memories.'

Hobson remained cold and impassive, but his partner became suddenly animated. 'You miss the point, sir! There is much crime on our streets. People have been robbed in broad daylight.' He shook his index finger to make his point. 'And it is all because of the devil's brew.'

'Hear! Hear!' Hobson said, nodding his head.

Tweeding stared at Micawber with loathing, and added, 'And it has been brought to our attention that many weeks ago another article of yours was published about horse racing. First gambling, now alcohol addiction. What other vices will you be endorsing in your writings?'

'Fornication, I shouldn't wonder,' Hobson said quietly, and then looked as if he had been tainted by the use of the word.

'Nonsense!' Micawber thundered. 'My next journalistic endeavour will wholly satisfy you worthy gentlemen. It will be an essay on tea and coffee drinking. Think of the extra revenue your establishment will accrue once my readers begin to feel the need for light refreshment, because my pen can be persuasive indeed—'

'Good afternoon, sir,' Tweeding interrupted. 'You have taken up enough of our time.'

He walked to the side of the window and tugged on a wide cord that dangled from the ceiling. It must have rung a bell in another room, because seconds later the door opened and the elderly man appeared.

'Uncle Wilfred,' Hobson said, 'will you escort this gentleman off the premises?'

With as much dignity as he could muster, Micawber walked towards the door. But Hobson's chosen words, treating him as if he was some sort of felon, had upset him.

He turned at the door and commanded their attention. 'I will bid you good afternoon, gentlemen. I shall return to my domicile, whereupon I will consume a glass of refreshing port wine. And I shall feel none the worse for it. None the worse!'

22

Micawber's Next Step

As Young Wilkins folded another garment and packed it carefully in the trunk, he heard his mother sniffing loudly and turned to see if she was still weeping. She appeared to be over the worst of it, but still dabbed at the corners of her eyes with a lace handkerchief and swallowed noisily.

'Please don't worry about me, Mama. Sydney is no distance when you consider how far we have travelled from England.'

His mother cast her eyes around his small bedroom and gestured at the four walls with her handkerchief. 'But your room, Young Wilkins, how shall I endure such emptiness?'

'It may not be empty for very long.'

'Of course: Emma will no longer have to share with the twins and can move in here.'

'Perhaps,' Young Wilkins said with an enigmatic smile. 'And then again, perhaps not.'

Mrs Micawber frowned. 'Whatever do you mean?'

Changing the subject hastily, Young Wilkins said, 'I wonder where Papa is? He's been gone most of the afternoon. I hope Tweeding and Hobson see his potential as a loyal employee.'

For some reason she couldn't quite fathom, Mrs Micawber felt despondent about her husband's prospects. It was a worry that was deeply embedded in her mind, and there was no concrete reason for her anxiety. In the past, she had always been dedicated in her support of his abilities, but this time her intuition suggested there would be problems; and if asked to explain this lack of certainty that all would go well at Tweeding and Hobson, she would have been unable to provide a rational explanation.

Seeing the doubt written on his mother's face, Young Wilkins embraced her. 'Try not to worry. I am certain Papa will turn up trumps. And even if Tweeding and Hobson prove themselves unworthy of employing someone of his distinction, then I think – after his second article was published in this week's *Chronicle* – he may well find his inky career belongs not as a humble clerk but as a man of letters.'

His mother sighed deeply. 'Permanent employment and a regular income would have been the solution to our problems, whereas writing for the newspapers remains precarious.'

'Ah, but!' Young Wilkins said, releasing his mother from the embrace, and pacing the small, sparsely furnished room, his finger pointing skywards. 'Now that he has had several articles published, perhaps the editor will see fit to offer him a permanent position.'

'That would be the answer to our prayers. If Wilkins should return from Tweeding and Hobson in a crestfallen disposition, I will suggest a visit to the *Melbourne Chronicle*.'

Young Wilkins was about to ask his mother if she had a reason to doubt his father would not return with good news, when there was a forceful two bangs on the front door. They froze, staring nervously into each other's eyes, knowing that the knocking code that signified friend rather than foe was one knock, followed by a pause, three quick knocks, another pause, and then two slow knocks.

'Don't answer it,' Mrs Micawber whispered.

'I wasn't going to,' her son countered. 'Any idea who it might be?'

Mrs Micawber did a mental calculation before she answered. 'It might be Mr Crestfall about the piano, or it could be the butcher about his bill. His credit extends for barely two weeks.'

Again there came a thunderous two knocks.

Mrs Micawber whispered urgently, 'They eventually get tired of banging and go away. I only hope and pray that your papa does not choose to return home within the next ten minutes.'

Mrs Micawber need not have worried about this dire event taking place, because her husband was at that very moment sitting in Mr Kynoch's office at the *Melbourne Chronicle*, as if her suggestion to approach the editor about seeking employment on a permanent basis had reached Micawber in an extrasensory way.

But Micawber's visit to the editor was for another reason entirely.

When Micawber had been unceremoniously evicted from Tweeding and Hobson's establishment, he had walked along Rourke Street dejectedly, smarting from the indignity of the way he had been asked to leave their premises. Even Hobson's wretched uncle had treated him as if he was a convict from Van Diemen's Land.

What buzzed around in his head were irritating and unnecessary feelings of humiliation, and his sensibilities veered from anger to a self-congratulatory belief of having exposed his two interviewers to ridicule with his erudite exposition on tolerance. And as for his parting shot about consuming a glass of port....

But this, Micawber realized, was self-delusional, and when he thought about the overall effect his visit had had on Messrs Tweeding and Hobson, he came to the resounding conclusion that he had fared the worse from the experience.

As he dodged through the crowds thronging Melbourne's busy streets, he decided to wipe the memory of Tweeding and Hobson clean from his mind. He needed another plan, another option, to fall back on.

Suddenly, like a bright light illuminating the creative side of his brain, he had the answer, and hurried towards the offices of the *Melbourne Chronicle*.

At first the editor said he was too busy to see him, but when he thought about the published essay and its seasonal and nostalgic appeal to his readers, he relented, and offered Micawber ten minutes of his time if he returned half an hour later.

Micawber spent the next thirty minutes wandering aimlessly along Collins Street, now and then doffing his hat to anyone whose eye he caught (a strange creature, they thought), and stopping to admire some of the new buildings that had sprung up in this rapidly growing city.

When he returned to the newspaper offices precisely half an hour later, the editor asked if he wouldn't mind waiting another five minutes because he had an important problem to sort out. While he waited, Micawber availed himself of pencil and paper placed on the counter for the benefit of customers wishing to place advertisements in the newspaper. His brow creased in concentration, Micawber scribbled hurriedly, making alterations, crossing out and starting again. When he read what he had written back to himself, and was satisfied with the result, he tucked the paper inside his pocket. And just in time, because the editor called for him to enter his office, and he was a man who didn't like to be kept waiting.

Mr Kynoch, whose fair skin was red and blotched from sun and insect bites, sat slumped into his chair behind his desk, fanning himself with a pamphlet. He gestured for Micawber to take a seat in front of him.

Micawber flopped into a creaking chair, pleased of the respite after having walked around in the heat, and expelled air noisily, to show Kynoch he was a fellow sufferer.

'Aye,' Kynoch nodded, 'when I lived near Inverness, I thought I'd like to get away from cold wet weather, and all those midges that bite one in the summer. And here I am, out of the frying pan, as they say.'

Micawber was about to participate with what he often referred to as 'a smidgeon of small talk', but Kynoch got straight to the point.

'Now then, Mr Micawber, I see you are not carrying any of your journalistic endeavours this time, so what is your reason for this visit?'

'I have rather an astounding proposition to put to you. As you are aware, my second article was published this morning—'

Kynoch put up a hand to stop him. 'I think I may have mentioned on several occasions that I will not be taking on any more permanent staff.'

'That is not why I'm here to see you, Mr Kynoch.'

'Oh?' Kynoch's eyebrows rose, and there was a guarded suspicion in his voice.

'Perhaps I should explain. I have just come from a meeting with Messrs Tweeding and Hobson for a discussion about seeking employment as a shipping clerk starting in the New Year.'

'You mean, they were interviewing you for a job.'

'Quite. And I have to say I was unprepared for the greeting I received. To describe them as hostile would be to underestimate their attitude towards me. The intensity of their antipathy was unexpected and shocking.'

Kynoch snorted, and he tried but failed to suppress a grin. Momentarily confused, Micawber's mouth fell open.

'Do forgive me, Mr Micawber,' the editor said, attempting a serious look, although his eyes still shone with amusement. 'But please let me guess at what happened to ruin your interview. Tweeding and Hobson had read your article which was published in this week's edition of our newspaper, yes?'

'That is correct. But how could you possibly know...?' Micawber began.

'Those two gentlemen are teetotal, and think that everyone else should take the pledge. They are intolerant of anyone who touches a drop of liquor, however modest their consumption.'

'How do you know this?'

'It's common knowledge.'

'Not to me it wasn't. Although my rent collector was about to impart some information about them, and I suspect the topic may have been to do with their disposition regarding intoxicants.'

Micawber stretched his arms out towards the editor, appealing to his common sense.

'I ask you, what is wrong with wetting one's whistle from time to time?'

'I'm with you there, Mr Micawber. There is nothing I like better at the end of each day than to settle down with a wee dram. *Uisge beatha.*'

Micawber looked up at the ceiling as he tried to recall where he had heard the expression before. He gave up, and appealed to Kynoch.

'I'm afraid you have me at a disadvantage.'

'*Uisge beatha*, meaning the water of life.'

'Ah yes! Scotch whisky.'

Kynoch glanced at the pocket watch that lay on the desk beside him, and then his eyes narrowed as he peered at Micawber. 'You mentioned some sort of proposition.'

'Because of the article that was published in your journal, the world of commerce has rejected my flair for administration and bookkeeping.'

'I hope you're not suggesting that was my fault.'

'No. It was I who found Bacchanalian inspiration in the observance of Yuletide and composed the incriminating essay. Your newspaper was merely the catalyst in my reluctant withdrawal from commerce and is therefore blameless. However, the potential employment with Tweeding and Hobbs, which has now vanished because of my impulsive journalism, was a mere stepping stone, thus bringing me to the conclusion that I should now proceed with the stratagem that eluded me until my most unfortunate encounter with our abstemious gentlemen. In short, I have another plan up my sleeve!'

'Go on,' Kynoch said in a subdued tone, fighting the urge to ask his visitor to get to the point. He was feeling charitable. Not only had he grown rather fond of Micawber, whose avuncular eccentricity was strangely appealing, his festive article had been the subject of much positive discussion.

'I require your assistance in placing an advertisement in your esteemed journal,' Micawber said. 'And I regret I am temporarily short of funds.' He pointed a finger upwards for emphasis. 'But of this I am certain: the advertisement will prove to be advantageous for both your humble servant and your respected periodical.'

'And what do you wish to advertise in the classified section of our esteemed organ?'

Micawber wasn't entirely certain, but he could have sworn the editor's tone was slightly mocking. But at least he seemed to be in a good mood so Micawber felt far from discouraged.

'I wish to advertise my services as a detective. A private inquiry agent.'

There was a long pause while Micawber's declaration was digested by Kynoch, who thought his visitor's personality had made a leap beyond eccentricity.

'I am told I have the aptitude for it,' Micawber added.

'Have you any experience in the field of detection?' Kynoch asked, once he had recovered and wiped the expression of incredulity from his face.

'Not as such. But when challenged by duplicity and legerdemain, my skills at reasoning, using the sciences of logic and deduction, give me cogent solutions to most riddles. I will provide you with an example. My twins asked me a riddle which I solved in a matter of minutes. I will now tell you the same riddle and I challenge you to solve it.'

Kynoch glanced at his watch again. 'Providing it isn't too long.'

Licking his lips in anticipation, Micawber proceeded with his story. 'A man went upstairs, turned off the light, and then went to bed. The next morning, while he breakfasted, there was a knock on the door, and he was surprised that the police had come to arrest him because he was responsible for the death of hundreds of people. Why was that?'

Kynoch shrugged. 'I have no idea.'

Irritation crept into Micawber's tone. 'Well, think about it. Try to guess.'

'Very well. The man went to bed. Could he have walked in his sleep and unwittingly shot people with a gun?'

Micawber suddenly felt annoyed. It was not the correct solution, but Kynoch had somehow managed to find a logical way to solve the riddle.

'No, no!' Micawber said impatiently. 'That is not the answer.'

'Well, it is *an* answer, and it makes perfect sense.'

'Nonsense. The blast from the gun would have woken him up and he would have known he was responsible for killing people. I said the man was surprised when the police called.'

'Very well. I give up. What is the answer?'

Micawber grinned triumphantly. 'The man was a lighthouse keeper. He went upstairs and turned off the light. So, you see, a ship ran aground on the rocks, killing hundreds of people. It was because of his negligence that they died.'

'But solving a child's riddle does not mean you can pursue criminals like an experienced detective.'

'Why not? When I solved the riddle I detected the truth behind it. Detection is about arriving at a solution.'

'That's all very well but ... supposing I agree to insert an advertisement, you mentioned something about a quid pro quo. What benefit will there be for my newspaper?'

Micawber leant forward in his seat, his excitement growing now that he knew his fish was hooked. 'I will offer the *Melbourne Chronicle* exclusive rights to publish my true life tales and exploits as a detective.'

Kynoch thought about this. He didn't think Micawber would be taken seriously and employed as a detective, but as it was close to Christmas and he was feeling benevolent, what harm was there in giving him a few sentences in the personal column?

'As we are a weekly newspaper, I agree to give you two insertions; one next week and one the following week. After that, any further insertions will have to be paid for. Now, have you thought about what you would like to say in this advertisement?'

Micawber rummaged in his pocket for the paper on which he had composed his advertisement and handed it to Kynoch. The editor's eyes scanned it from top to bottom, frowning deeply as he read words like 'intrepid', 'conundrum' and 'enigma'. He looked at his smiling visitor and said, 'This is rather too wordy for an advert in the personal column, Mr Micawber.'

'Yes but—' Micawber began.

'No "buts" about it,' Kynoch interrupted. 'I know newspapers, and we want something concise and to the point.'

'Pithy?' Micawber suggested.

'Exactly. Something like: "Private Detective will unravel mysteries and solve your problems. Discretion Guaranteed. Can be contacted at...." Followed by your address. That should do the trick.'

Micawber leapt to his feet, stretched across the desk, clasped Kynoch's right hand in both of his and shook it wildly. 'Thank you, Mr Kynoch. You won't be sorry for performing this philanthropic act.'

He released Kynoch's hand and walked to the door where he turned to deliver an exit speech.

'Once again the *Melbourne Chronicle* demonstrates a progressive attitude in its selection of anecdotal material; true tales of high quality which I hope to compile about my escapades in solving mysteries, and I am certain these narratives will make numerical increases in the vending of your periodical. In short, I hope they may boost your circulation. Good-day to you, Mr Kynoch.'

Mr Kynoch sank back in his seat and blew out his cheeks. He always felt exhausted by Micawber's visits, and was glad he would be home in less than an hour, where he would reward himself with a not so wee dram.

23

Young Wilkins, Actor

As SOON AS Micawber arrived home he found his wife and son in the parlour. Young Wilkins stood by the window, reading a copy of *Hamlet*, his lips silently mouthing lines from the play, and Mrs Micawber was sitting on the *chaise-longue*, a work basket at her feet, darning a pile of clothes that needed remedial treatment before further deterioration.

When she looked up and saw the happy smile on her husband's face, she cried, 'Wilkins! I can see by the expression on your face that the meeting was successful. What a shame you will not be shouldering your responsibilities before the New Year. But at least we face the coming year with prospects which are clement, having weathered the current climate of privation.'

Mr Micawber shook his head rapidly, his jowls rippling as he adopted a more serious expression. 'I fear Tweeding and Hobson missed an opportunity to enhance the quality of their human assets, thus improving the financial prospects of their establishment. In short, they did not offer me the job.'

Mrs Micawber gasped. 'Why, Wilkins? Why?'

Micawber described the interview in detail. After he had finished speaking, Young Wilkins snapped his book shut.

'Never mind, Papa! You would not wish to work for employers whose disapproval of harmless pleasures would intrude on your personal tastes.'

'But I don't understand,' Mrs Micawber said, addressing her

husband. 'You walked through that door looking as happy as a child with a bag of bonbons.'

The smile returned to Micawber's face. 'I was mightily pleased with some consolatory news. But when you asked me about Tweeding and Hobson, naturally I thought it of prime importance you heard the adverse revelations before proceeding with the good news. After the unproductive meeting with Tweeding and Hobson, I decided to pay Mr Kynoch a visit, the esteemed editor of the *Melbourne Chronicle*.'

'And he's offered you a permanent post?'

'If you'll allow me to finish, My Dear. No, he has not offered me a position with his newspaper. He has, however, agreed to allow me to advertise in his personal column gratis. Two free insertions, he said.'

'But what will you advertise?'

Micawber pressed a thumb into one of his coat pockets, his fingers splayed on the outside, and with his other hand he gripped the jacket collar on his chest, adopting what he thought was a fitting stance for his new occupation.

'You are looking at Wilkins Micawber, Detective.'

Young Wilkins looked pleased with himself. 'Capital! You decided to adopt my suggestion. I knew you would.'

Mrs Micawber felt a tremor of panic in her stomach. 'But what if you should encounter murderers, larcenists and all manner of criminals? Or even worse, what if nobody replies to your advertisement?'

Young Wilkins chuckled. 'Don't worry unduly, Mama. I am certain someone somewhere will want an investigation undertaken for some minor infringement. So I'm sure Papa will be quite safe. And please do not worry about finances. I have already given you one piece of good news regarding my prospects as an actor—'

'An actor!' Micawber shouted. 'When did this happen?'

'I wanted it to be a surprise. I will be working for Mr George

Coppin, and joining his company in Sydney. I leave first thing tomorrow by stagecoach.' He held the copy of the play up to his father. 'My first role will be Horatio in *Hamlet*.'

Micawber's eyes glistened as he took this in, and then he grabbed his son by the shoulders. 'I could not have wished for a better beginning for my son's illustrious career. Well done, My Boy! At least someone in our family has found a placement.'

Mrs Micawber let out a sound that was both a sigh and a low moan. 'If only Young Wilkins did not have to stray so far from home.'

'Less than five hundred miles,' Young Wilkins assured her. 'And before long I think there might well run a railway between these two cities. But I haven't told you the other part of the good news, which I was going to save for tomorrow, until Godfrey arrives to explain his offer to you.'

Frowning, Micawber stepped back and regarded his son questioningly. 'Offer?'

Young Wilkins grinned. 'Yes, and this should be a solution to your immediate monetary problems, Papa.'

'How so?'

'Well, the man whose shack Godfrey lived in and looked after in Canvas Town has struck gold up at Mount Korong. Therefore he no longer needs his shack and he has given it to Godfrey.'

'But how will this benefit our family?'

Young Wilkins's smile widened. 'Godfrey thinks he can sell the shack for more than twenty pounds. And, as I will be leaving for Sydney, there is no reason why Godfrey shouldn't be your tenant. He can have my old room and pay you rent for it.'

The intake of breath from both Mr and Mrs Micawber filled the room with optimism.

'This is most heartening and promising,' Micawber said, and turned to his wife. 'This may be the answer to all our prayers, and I can't think of a more agreeable soul than young Godfrey McNeil. He will be made most welcome in our humble domicile.'

Mrs Micawber nodded vigorously. 'He is such a kind gentleman. I think our fortune has already changed for the better.'

Micawber smacked his lips and his eyes alighted on the empty decanter.

'Perhaps, as we are now unshackled from chains of hardship, there will be funds for occasional indulgences which make life bearable.'

'Hold your horses, Papa!' Young Wilkins said. 'While it may seem as if Godfrey is a benefactor, please consider his position as a paying tenant. His contribution to the rent and household expenses should be a fair and equal proportion.'

'Of course, of course,' Micawber replied. 'I am sure we will come to an equitable arrangement. And if the carrot that I dangle in the personal column of the *Melbourne Chronicle* achieves a propitious outcome, then our Christmas will be spent in clover.'

'Alas!' Young Wilkins exclaimed. 'My deepest regret in leaving for Sydney is that I will not be spending Christmas with my parents.'

His father patted him on the arm. 'Our very first Christmas without Young Wilkins. It will not be the same.'

Mrs Micawber sniffed, and both son and husband looked at her, thinking that she was on the verge of tears; but they noticed that she had drifted off into some distant reverie.

'What is it, My Dear?' Micawber asked.

'I was thinking of Emma.'

'Oh! But what she has not possessed she will not miss.'

'What are you talking about, Wilkins?'

'I mean, Emma will not – now that Young Godfrey is joining us – be moving out of the twins' room into Young Wilkins's old room.'

'When I said I was thinking of Emma, it had nothing to do with her sleeping arrangements. I was pondering Christmas Day, and wondered where she will be spending it, now that she is betrothed to Ridger Begs.'

'You think Mr and Mrs Begs will invite her to spend Christmas with them?'

'Perhaps,' Young Wilkins broke in, 'they will invite all of the Micawber family to spend the festive day with them.'

There was a silence, while husband and wife exchanged looks, both frowning. The thoughts of spending Christmas Day with the Begs lacked appeal, mainly because of the constricting feelings of guilt regarding the debt to their landlord.

Noticing his parents' lack of enthusiasm, and possibly guessing the cause, Young Wilkins slapped his hands together to gain their attention.

'Never mind that now,' he said, smiling. 'You can worry about that nearer the time. For now I would like us to celebrate my departure for pastures new and a prolific career treading the boards.'

Micawber looked woefully at the decanter. 'I fear the vessel of celebration has run dry.'

Young Wilkins laughed and waved his father's gloom aside. 'Mr Coppin has advanced me expenses so that I can secure accommodation in Sydney. If I'm careful, I think I may be able slip into the amount and remove just enough to purchase fresh wine and some victuals for this evening.'

'By Jove, Young Wilkins! This will be a celebration indeed!'

24

A Disagreement

Now THAT THE young lovers were betrothed, Mrs Begs felt it was unnecessary to chaperone them, and left them to their own devices on the terrace overlooking the garden. She had at first been reluctant to allow them time on their own, not because she feared any impropriety, but because of her son's lack of social graces and conversation. She had no illusions about his limited social skills and fretted that he might bore his fiancée with conversation which she knew was esoteric, and Emma would have little or no interest in hearing about his hunting exploits.

His father was away on business in Adelaide and he had been left in charge of his affairs, knowing this was to be an assessment of his competence to run the family business; but there was something buried deep in his mind, a spectral stirring, telling him that he lacked his father's business acumen. It was the first time he had been left in charge of the family business, and he knew he had to prove himself worthy but felt he was floundering.

Earlier in the day he had attended a meeting with Mr Larkfield about their properties, and the subject of the Micawbers' tenancy had arisen. Larkfield had let slip that Micawber and his wife and son had recently spent the night at the theatre, and surely their priority was in paying their debts before gratifying their desire for mild entertainment. This put Ridger in a position of wanting to defend his future in-laws, but at the same time he wanted to show Larkfield that he was not a man to be trifled with.

'The Micawbers can move to Canvas Town, for all I care,' he had said; adding rather harshly, when he saw the surprised expression on Larkfield's face, which he interpreted as approval that he was no longer weak-minded, 'And the sooner the better.'

As they lay next to each other in reclining chairs, Emma with a parasol to keep the sun's harsh rays off her delicate skin, Ridger squinted in the glare and felt the heat was making him even more irritable than his encounter with Larkfield. Usually he was physically occupied, dashing about and rarely still. Now he felt his face burning, because for the last half-hour he had been sitting completely still listening to Emma telling him the story of *Pride and Prejudice* by Jane Austen, which she had recently finished reading.

'What did you think of the story?' she asked him.

He blinked his eyes open and tried to recall what she had told him about Mr Bennett and his five daughters, one of whom is in love with Mr Darcy, but for some reason Ridger couldn't quite make out, rejects him, and eventually becomes engaged to the man.

'I think it's interesting,' he admitted grudgingly, and couldn't resist adding after a long pause. 'But ...'

'But?' Emma questioned.

'Not much happens between – what's her name?'

'Elizabeth Bennett.'

'Between Elizabeth Bennett not liking Darcy and then liking him. I think the mark of a good yarn is something adventurous happening, like a fight or a duel or something.'

Emma found it hard to summon up the patience needed to explain about the intricacies of the characters' relationships, and her voice had a brittle edge to it.

'Stories that might appeal to young boys, you mean.'

This criticism, coupled with the brooding thoughts about her parents' profligacy, succeeded in turning the usually placid young man into an irrational bully. He sat up and stared at her with such loathing that she felt scared.

'Boring! That's what that story was. Boring! You and your family do nothing but useless prattling. It's time you all shut up.'

An angry fleck of spittle smeared his lower lip and his complexion was a blazing red beacon. She had never seen this side of him before and she was frightened, and couldn't help wondering what life would be like once they were married.

'I'm sorry,' she said, her voice parched and tremulous. 'I just thought—'

She didn't get a chance to finish. She found his finger pointing inches away from her face.

'I told you to shut up! And when I say shut up, I mean shut up. I never want to hear one of your stupid stories again. Is that clear?'

She nodded mutely. And then she noticed the tears welling up in his eyes and she began to feel sorry for him. She tried to take his hand in hers, but he snatched it away. He stood up abruptly, so that her parasol masked his face, for he didn't want her to notice the tears. Tears were for babies and children. Men didn't cry. It was unmanly, and he felt ashamed of his weakness and hated her for causing him to behave in this unmasculine way.

'I'll go and find Jimmy and get him to take you home.'

She turned and watched his retreating figure hurrying towards the back of the house to fetch the coachman. His stride indicated a determination to be decisive now that he was set on a course of action.

It was their first disagreement, and it seemed to have arrived from nowhere. She had merely made a remark that in most circumstances would not have warranted such a savage reaction and it worried her deeply. It was intensely unsettling and she began to agonize about their relationship, wondering if she had done the right thing in agreeing to marry him, because in the back of her mind a voice suggested that she had agreed to marry into the Begs family for the sake of her own family, who needed some financial stability.

But this, she realized, was sacrificing her one chance of happiness. She doubted she could ever really be happy spending a lifetime with Ridger Begs and he had just given her a demonstration of what the future could be like.

25

The Lodger

'I WISH YOU the best luck in the world, My Boy,' said a misty-eyed Micawber. 'And I will look forward to seeing you "treading the boards" when Mr George Coppin's company returns to Melbourne.'

The stagecoach horses shook their heads and snorted as if they were anxious to be on their way, and their harnesses jangled and creaked. Young Wilkins took a deep breath and hefted his trunk onto a shoulder and up to one of the drivers on top of the coach, who forced it into a tight slot between other items of luggage and secured all of them with several leather straps.

It was almost time to leave. Mrs Micawber dabbed her eyes with her best silk handkerchief which she had brought with her for this bitterly sweet occasion. Her fledgling was fleeing the nest, which she knew was inevitable, but she was determined to indulge in the melancholy of her son's departure, secure in the knowledge that he would probably be returning to Melbourne before very long, but as an itinerant actor, for he was now destined to spend the rest of his life touring from town to town.

'We are all going to miss you,' she said; 'especially Emma and the twins.'

'And I shall miss them. Please give them another big hug from me, Mama.'

Emma, Emily and Edward had said their farewells at home, all of them sad and tearful, but also excited because their big brother might one day become a famous actor like Mr Macready.

'Before you leave us, Young Wilkins,' – Micawber leaned forward conspiratorially and lowered his voice – 'there is something I have been meaning to ask you.'

Young Wilkins raised an enquiring eyebrow, one of the expressions he had been practising.

'When you performed for me Hamlet's soliloquy, I thought the performance was most credible, and I could understand and was moved by the prince's agony, but – and I hope you will not take this unfavourably – I felt an audience would demand a more lavish and corporeal presentation.'

Young Wilkins didn't mind the criticism and chuckled goodnaturedly. 'You're quite right, Papa. And when I performed personally for Mr Coppin that is exactly what I did. You see, when I was instructed by Godfrey to think about Hamlet's internal strife, rather than posturing and gesturing, I was transformed into giving a performance that was far more realistic than I had ever considered giving previously. And it was all with Godfrey's help, for he told me that once I had practised and got to grips with the inner struggle of each character, that is the time to expand in a more physical sense.'

'It is uncanny how well instructed Young Godfrey is in the thespian arts. Are you sure he hasn't "trod the boards" himself?'

'He denies ever having done so.'

'Curious,' Micawber pondered with a deep frown.

'And talking of Godfrey, where is the scoundrel? He was supposed to be here to see my departure; and more importantly to accompany you back to his new lodgings.'

'All aboard!' one of the drivers commanded.

The stagecoach was not one of the 'leviathans' that operated between Ballarat and Geelong, but a smaller American, more comfortably sprung type, one of the many operated by the Californian entrepreneur, Freeman Cobb. There were four other passengers for Sydney, a bearded man and his wife and daughter, and a short, overweight young man, dressed all in black.

Young Wilkins scanned the street, his hand on the open door of the coach as the other passengers climbed aboard. And then he spotted Godfrey's head, bobbing along Collins Street, carrying a brown battered case on his shoulders, weaving in and out of the crowds.

'All aboard!' the driver repeated, this time with more urgency for Young Wilkins's benefit.

Young Wilkins looked up at him. 'Just thirty seconds more, I beg you.'

The coachman, an American, shook his head. 'We have a reputation to consider. Either you get on board or you stay here.'

Reluctantly, Wilkins put one foot on the step just as Godfrey arrived breathlessly, dropping his baggage on the ground. He grabbed his friend's hand and shook it.

'I cannot begin to tell you how much I envy you your journey, Wilkins.'

'I can't think why. The rocking motion sometimes causes a sea sickness.'

The coachman could see this conversation escalating and snapped, 'Time to depart. This is your last chance.'

Young Wilkins loosened his grip on Godfrey's hand and pulled himself up into the vehicle, turning to speak to his friend through the open window.

'I wasn't speaking about envying you this journey,' Godfrey explained hurriedly. 'I meant your journey of discovery as you explore each character in your performances. I wish you all success. I hope you have better luck than I did.'

Young Wilkins's mouth fell open. 'But you told me you have never acted before.'

Godfrey smiled knowingly and winked at his friend. Then the crack of a whip, and the coach heaved and jerked, and Young

Wilkins just had time to give his parents a quick wave before the coach departed along Collins Street.

Mrs Micawber used her handkerchief to alternate between dabbing her eyes and waving, and Mr Micawber held his cane aloft, sweeping it in a broad gesture from side to side.

'God go with you and guide you, my precious boy,' Mrs Micawber called.

As he watched the departing stagecoach, Micawber's spirits sank into a mixture of disappointment and yearning. He wasn't jealous of his son and, more than anything he could wish for at this moment, wanted him to succeed, but he envied him his vocation. How Micawber would have liked to strut through a stage door, sit in a theatre dressing room applying greasepaint, preparing for a momentous performance. Somehow the vicarious pleasure of Young Wilkins's opportunity seemed lame compared to his own ambitious dreams. But that was all they were. Dreams.

Noticing Micawber's gloomy countenance and naturally thinking it was to do with the parting (which it was, mostly), Godfrey said, 'Please don't feel sad about his departure. I have a feeling your son has a promising future before him, and he may soon be so rich he will be able to care for his family like the devoted son he is.'

Micawber hadn't considered this aspect of his son's success story and began to feel enormously optimistic. He placed a paternal hand on Godfrey's shoulder.

'Our firstborn may have flown to the Temple of Thespis, but we rejoice in welcoming you as his true friend into the bosom of our family, and this mutually beneficial arrangement will defend us from the enforcement of monetary liabilities. In short, you have saved our bacon!'

Godfrey accepted this encouraging speech with a toothy smile. 'I will be glad to help in any way I can.'

'And now let us turn around and direct our steps towards your new place of residence, Master Godfrey.'

Godfrey picked up his bag, Micawber offered his wife an arm, and the three of them set off along Collins Street, weaving in and out of the crowds while attempting to hold a conversation while they walked.

'I will need to return to Canvas Town this afternoon,' Godfrey said, swerving to avoid bumping a well-dressed lady with his bag, 'to hand my shack over to the new purchaser. I managed to obtain twenty-two guineas for it.'

'Splendid, Godfrey! Splendid!'

'As soon as we arrive, perhaps we can sit down and discuss my rent as your lodger, and also any contribution I might make to the household costs.'

'All in good time, my dear chap,' Micawber said, who felt business and bargaining between friends needed no discomfiting discussion.

As soon as they had left Collins Street, heading north-east, the crowds thinned. Godfrey was silent for a while, deep in thought, and even Micawber had been silenced by thoughts of their sudden good fortune and was unaware of the small satisfied humming noises he was making.

'And where is your daughter?' Godfrey asked. 'She didn't come to see her brother depart.'

Mrs Micawber leaned forward as she walked and looked across her husband at Godfrey. 'Emma had to look after the twins and take them for their schooling. They all bade their brother farewell and embraced him at home. She should be back there by the time we return.'

'Good,' Godfrey said. 'I really look forward to seeing Emma again.'

The familiarity with which he said this was not lost on either Mr or Mrs Micawber, and both frowned in unison. It was unspoken, but both of them preferred Godfrey to Ridger, who was a far more personable young man, and would have been a much better match for their daughter. If it were not for one shortcoming, which they both tried to sweep from the forefront of their minds, denying that wealth and social standing had anything to do with it.

26

Emma Micawber's Strange Behaviour

AFTER SETTLING INTO his new lodgings, Godfrey went out in the afternoon to hand over the key to the padlock securing his shack in Canvas Town, and returned twenty-two guineas richer.

He gave Mr Micawber five pounds, for a month's rent and as a contribution towards food and essentials. Mr Micawber was delighted, as it saved him having to discuss such indelicate matters as money with a friend, although he was never reserved when it came to haggling with a tradesman or potential employers.

Feeling financially comfortable for the first time in many months, Micawber set off to purchase sundry items for their dinner that evening, which would be something of a celebration to welcome Godfrey as a guest in their home. His wife made him promise to visit the butcher and pay at least half of the outstanding bill (12/6d.) and also pay Pellinore Crestfall a sum that would satisfy him until after Christmas (it was agreed that £1.10s. might be adequate), and a few other sundry creditors.

After Micawber had left on his shopping expedition, and Mrs Micawber went to the kitchen to begin preparing vegetables to go with whatever meat would be placed steaming upon their table that evening, Godfrey settled himself into an easy chair in the parlour and began reading *Pride and Prejudice*, which Emma had left on top of the piano.

As he sat reading, he heard Mrs Micawber's voice raised in the kitchen, talking loudly to Emma. He thought at first they were quarrelling, until he heard Mrs Micawber urging her daughter to 'Please go in to the parlour and make our guest feel at home'.

A minute later, Emma entered, looking flushed and sheepish, catching Godfrey's eye momentarily, and then avoiding it as she sat opposite him on the *chaise-longue*. He remained silent, smiling and staring at her until she was forced to look up and catch his eye again.

'I'm sorry,' he said. 'When you entered I should have stood up. But you came in and sat down so quickly. And I was so engrossed in this book. Is it yours?'

Emma nodded.

'I have read *Sense and Sensibility*, and I thought the relationships between all the characters were most fascinating. Have you finished reading this book yet?'

When she answered him she experienced a strange sensation, hearing the tone of her own voice as if she was listening to someone else.

'I finished it last week. It was very good.'

'I should very much like to borrow this book. And then I can give you my opinion of it.'

Unlike Ridger, Godfrey seemed so self-assured that Emma felt an anger welling up inside her and was confused by this irrational emotion. Before she could stop herself she said, 'What can you possibly tell me about the book that I don't already know?'

Unperturbed by her dismissive attitude, Godfrey smiled and said, 'I shouldn't think I could tell you anything about the plot and characters with which you are not familiar. However, I could offer a critical viewpoint and it would be fascinating to debate the finer intricacies of the novel with you.'

'I'm afraid that will not be possible. You see my father hasn't read it yet, and he was about to read it on my recommendation.'

'Well, perhaps after your father has read it.'

Emma glanced at the carriage clock and stood up. 'If you will excuse me....'

Godfrey also rose hurriedly. 'If I have said anything to offend you ...'

'I have some correspondence to write, and I wish to attend to it in my room, that is all.'

Godfrey stared pointedly at the clock. 'It will soon be time to collect the twins from school. Perhaps I could accompany you again.'

'That won't be necessary.'

'But the streets of Melbourne—'

'The streets of Melbourne,' she interrupted, 'were the same six months ago, before we made your acquaintance, and I managed to accompany the twins without any problems. But thank you for your kind offer.'

She swept out of the parlour, leaving Godfrey grinning confidently, and thinking about the line from *Hamlet*, which he quoted under his breath.

'"The lady doth protest too much, methinks".'

Two days had gone by since Ridger had quarrelled with Emma. Feeling she was slipping away from him, and not knowing what he could do about it, he was unable to concentrate on running the family business. It was just as well his father was due to return from Adelaide later that day because things were not going well.

His mother found him unable to eat breakfast and sunk into the deepest gloom. At once her instinct told her that the cause of his suffering was something to do with his fiancée rather than the business.

She poured herself tea and sat near him at the enormous table. He shifted awkwardly in his seat, knowing she was going to question him about Emma. He was torn between wanting to keep their quarrel to himself and seeking his mother's advice.

'Emma was here two days ago, she left in a hurry, without

saying goodbye to me,' Mrs Begs observed, 'and you haven't mentioned seeing her again. Is something wrong?'

Ridger shrugged, pouted and stared at his uneaten plate of eggs and kidneys.

'Well?' his mother prompted.

'We had a disagreement.'

'About what?'

'Oh, nothing important.'

'It must have been about something.'

'Something minor. Hardly worth mentioning.'

Mrs Begs put two sugar lumps in her tea and stirred. The clinking of the teaspoon in the early morning silence jarred her son's nerves. She watched as he squirmed beneath her gaze. Eventually, the silence got the better of him.

'She was telling me about the story of a book she had read. Afterwards I told her I didn't think it was much of a story, and she said something about it not being interesting to boys. And I felt—'

Ridger stopped speaking as he searched for the appropriate word.

'Insecure?' offered his mother.

He nodded. 'And that was when I told her I never wanted to hear another story, and all her family did was prattle.'

Mrs Begs startled her son with an amused laugh. 'Oh, is that all? As you said, Ridger, it was a minor quarrel. And what couple doesn't go through arguments like that in a relationship. Your father and I had many such disagreements when we were courting.'

Ridger's brows contracted into a deep frown. He had neglected to describe to his mother the severity of his anger, the way he had frightened Emma by his viciousness, leaving her in no doubt that he could resort to violence.

'Is there something more? Something you're not telling me?'

Ridger shook his head.

'Are you sure about that?'

'I've told you everything. It's just – it's just that I said it in such an angry way, I may have frightened her.'

'I see,' Mrs Begs said, and remained silent for a moment while she thought about the scene that had taken place between Emma and her son. She understood how Emma would feel; the way Ridger probably terrified her with a glimpse into the future as his wife. Naturally, as his mother, Mrs Begs had witnessed his white-hot temper on many occasions when he was a child. Sometimes his tantrums had been extremely violent and his father had threatened to beat him on many occasions; but he could never bring himself to do it, mainly because of his own experiences in the workhouse when he himself was a child, knowing how a beating did little to alter his behaviour in any way, and, if anything, made him more resolute in his bitterness and gave him more grounds for revenge.

Although she supported her husband in his reluctance to resort to corporal punishment to correct her son's behaviour, Mrs Begs also realized that her son soon became aware that his father's threats were hollow and his behaviour did not get any better. If only, she thought, her husband had administered one sound thrashing, her son's behaviour might have improved, because any future threats would have had some impact. And, although his behaviour had improved as a youth, there were still occasions when his temper went so out of control, as if his brain was possessed by demons, that she worried he might one day kill someone.

On the other hand, since he had matured there were less violent occurrences, which she believed was the result of his phys-ical pursuits, such as hunting. And she had never known him to show anything but consideration towards the opposite sex. So perhaps his relationship with Emma was not beyond repair, espe-cially as his contrition seemed so sincere.

'Ridger,' she said after a long and uncomfortable pause, 'when you lost your temper with Emma, no doubt it was because you felt slighted in some way. I think it is because you have a passionate, sensitive nature. And provided you are telling me the absolute truth about not resorting to violence—'

Ridger shook his head emphatically, and pulled a face to show his abhorrence of such an action.

'Then I think,' his mother continued, 'you mustn't leave it a minute longer. You must visit Emma as soon as possible. Why not call round this afternoon, and apologize to her? Explain to her that you would never hurt her in any physical sense. Tell her how you felt slighted. I'm sure she will understand.'

Ridger remained moodily silent, staring at his breakfast plate. Mrs Begs sighed loudly, her frustration being tested beyond the limit.

'Ridger! Pull yourself together! Emma will think far more of you if you explain exactly how you feel. And that I believe is the secret: sharing your feelings. Just explain to her how you feel.'

Ridger stared at his mother, uncertainty in his eyes. 'It's not just about our quarrel.'

'Then what is it?'

'I just feel so … I don't think we are equals. Emma knows so much that I don't. She reads books and can talk about all kinds of things. I'm worried about when we are married. Will she look down on me?'

Mrs Begs patted her son's hand. 'Everyone is different, Ridger. What about the stables behind the house? Remember how you almost built them yourself, with very little help from anyone else? Do you think Emma could have done that? And that time you almost broke Declan's record racing your father's favourite.'

'But I didn't actually break his record, did I?'

Mrs Begs smiled, knowing he was gradually coming round.

'No, but that's another thing Emma could not do; she could not race a horse at that speed. You both have different talents and skills, but that is as it should be. And Emma has always known that, so there is no reason for you to feel insecure.'

Suddenly the tension left Ridger's shoulders and his forehead resumed an expression of calm that had been absent for days. He picked up his knife and fork and began eating, much to his mother's satisfaction.

'You're right, Mother,' he said through a mouthful of kidney. 'I'll go round this afternoon. But this morning I'll do some hunting.'

'A good idea,' his mother smiled. 'Get it out of your system.'

27

Godfrey Plays His Cards Right

EYES CLOSED, HEAD tilted back, Godfrey listened attentively as Emma played Chopin's *Nocturne in G Minor*. A smile of contentment played at the corners of his mouth. He was in heaven. A pretty girl was playing the piano for him, and the notes were sweet and sentimental as her fingers caressed the keyboard. Once again, Godfrey imagined he was the recipient of those tender caresses.

But the reason Emma was playing the piano for him was to avoid conversation. Anything was better than having to confront what she knew in her heart was the awful truth: she was not in love with Ridger and was deeply attracted to Godfrey. And she knew Godfrey was about to make some sort of declaration of his feelings towards her; she had felt it building up and her feelings were divided into wanting it to happen and fear of the outcome. Up until now she had managed to avoid being in the same room alone with him, but Godfrey had left the house earlier to visit someone about some work as a compositor at the *Argus* newspaper – or so he said. Her parents had gone out a little while after Godfrey's departure, because her father thought a seaside stroll at St Kilda would blow away the cobwebs, and he also needed to purchase a copy of the next edition of the *Melbourne Chronicle*, in which his advertisement was due to appear. Only five minutes after they had left Godfrey returned under the pretext that he had left something behind in his room. She suspected it had not been a genuine mistake, and when she asked him about his visit to the *Argus* he dismissed it by saying it could wait until the afternoon. This convinced her that he had engineered the situation in which she found herself alone with him.

She reached the end of the nocturne and Godfrey opened his eyes and applauded her. She muttered her thanks and reached for another sheet of music on top of the piano, planning to perform another short piece. As she rifled through sheets of music, Godfrey seized the opportunity to declare his love for her, stood up and walked to her side.

'There is something I must tell you,' he said.

She avoided looking at him and mumbled, 'Please don't.'

She was saved by a knock on the door, someone using the agreed family code. Her mind shot through the limited possibilities of who was calling, and a cold hand gripped her by the throat. It could only be Ridger, of that she was certain. Godfrey, who now knew the code, was standing here beside her; her brother was in Sydney, the twins were at school and her parents had left for St Kilda. The only other person who knew the code was Ridger, because she had told him at their last fateful meeting, explaining that it was to do with security in these uncertain times, which was, she convinced herself, partly true.

'Shall I answer it?' Godfrey said.

A sharp intake of breath before Emma said, 'No! I had better go.'

By the fearful look on her face, Godfrey guessed it must be her fiancé calling. He returned to his seat to await the outcome, and he was also curious to see what her betrothed was like.

Emma, her blood pressure rising along with the colour in her face, dashed out to answer the door. As she unlatched and swung open the door, the look on her face was like that of someone exposed in a deceitful act, even though her innocence was not in any doubt; but Ridger was so immersed in his own feelings of remorse, he thought of nothing but the difficulties that lay ahead in finding the right words.

'I – I c-came to say I'm sorry about the other afternoon,' he stammered. 'It won't ever happen again. May I come in and we can talk it over?'

Emma's first thought was to find an excuse to keep him from entering and agree to meet him later, but what also flashed through her mind was a curiosity that needed to be satisfied about her fiancé's attitude in meeting their lodger.

Flushed and trembling slightly, she said, 'You had better come in.'

She led the way into the parlour. As soon as Ridger entered and saw Godfrey, his reaction was instantly hostile.

'Who the devil are you?'

Godfrey stood up and put out his hand, smiling pleasantly.

'This is Godfrey McNeil,' Emma said. 'I'd like you to meet my fiancé, Ridger Begs.'

Ignoring Godfrey's outstretched hand, Ridger scowled and turned to Emma, waiting for an explanation.

'Godfrey's our lodger.'

Ridger's forehead screwed into a puzzled frown. 'Lodger? Since when?'

'Since two days ago.'

'This house only has three bedrooms, so unless I'm mistaken—'

'If you'll allow me to explain,' Emma broke in. 'My brother has left to work as an actor in Sydney, and I share a room with the twins, so it seemed sensible for Godfrey, who is a friend of my brother, to occupy his room.'

Ridger threw Godfrey a suspicious glance before turning back to Emma. 'Why didn't you tell me this was going on?'

'I only found out about it two days ago when I returned from your house. My brother left early the next morning on the Sydney coach and Godfrey moved in later that morning. I was unable to tell you because when we parted company the other night—'

'Yes, well,' Ridger interrupted hastily, not wanting the other man to learn of their quarrel. 'That's why I called round. To sort things out.'

An awkward silence fell on the room. They heard a woman yelling something unintelligible in the street outside, followed by a loud crash and a scream, as if something had fallen from a wagon.

'Why don't we sit down?' Emma suggested. 'I could make us some tea.'

'I don't want any tea, thank you,' Ridger said, and sat hurriedly on the *chaise-longue*.

Emma looked enquiringly at Godfrey.

'Nor for me, thank you.'

Emma sat next to Ridger and Godfrey sank into a chair opposite. He offered Ridger a pleasant smile which was rejected by a glowering look. There followed another long pause which Emma was the first to break.

'Young Wilkins is working for George Coppin, the renowned actor,' she informed Ridger.

'I haven't heard of the man. But then I never go to the theatre. Waste of time.'

This boorish statement caused Emma to blush with embarrassment.

Godfrey sat back and studied Ridger with interest, his expression mild, but concealing his true thoughts. He thought Emma's fiancé was an oaf. That he was handsome was not in any doubt, but there was a simmering nastiness in his manner, and Godfrey decided that he had to be as forgiving as possible to this barbarian if he was to win Emma over.

'Well, we can't all like the same things,' Godfrey said, deliberately rescuing the oaf from further embarrassment. 'We are all very different.'

Ridger was thrown into confusion. The lodger's words echoed his mother's at breakfast, and they were clearly designed to be as understanding as possible, whereas he had been expecting some sort of contradiction, something he could get his teeth into. Unable to think of a reply, his attention focused on Emma's copy of *Pride and Prejudice* which lay on an occasional table nearby, and he grabbed at it like a drowning man.

'Ah! *Pride and Prejudice.* This is the story you were telling me.' He stared at Godfrey. 'Have you read this book?'

'No, but I have read several other Jane Austen novels.'

'And what did you think of them?'

'They are very clever; the wit is very sharp indeed.'

Emma, for reasons she couldn't explain to herself, but which she would later regret, said, 'Ridger thinks *Pride and Prejudice* is a very poor story, and perhaps more action, like a duel or something, might put some life into it.'

She felt her fiancé squirming at her side, but was surprised by Godfrey saying, 'I haven't read that particular novel, but I'm inclined to agree with your fiancé. A bit more action would certainly perk up Miss Austen's books.'

Emma was stunned by his reaction. She had thought Godfrey to be more cultured than Ridger, especially when she considered the way he had helped her brother with his interpretation of Hamlet.

'I don't have time to read,' Ridger declared. 'Life is far too busy for that. I have to help run our family business. And what business are you in, McNeil?'

It was Emma's turn to squirm, from the way Ridger boasted about the business to the way he questioned Godfrey with the clear intention of making him feel small.

'I am seeking employment at the moment,' Godfrey replied.

Coming to his rescue, Emma said, 'Mr McNeil has an interview this afternoon at the *Argus.*'

'Oh!' Ridger exclaimed with a sneer. 'So you're a writer too.'

'This is for work as a compositor.'

Ridger stared blankly at him.

'A compositor arranges the letters for the printing,' Godfrey explained, unable to disguise his patronizing tone.

Ridger flushed angrily. 'I know damn well what a compositor does, McNeil.'

Emma was shocked. 'Ridger! Mr McNeil was only trying to be helpful.'

'I'm sorry,' Godfrey said to Ridger, leaning forward with an expression of concern. 'I didn't mean to offend you in any way.'

But Ridger was angered by the way his fiancée seemed to be more favourably disposed towards her lodger, and his jealousy surfaced in a wave of hatred.

'I suppose you are aware that we own this dwelling in which you sit.'

Godfrey's face was inscrutable, but inwardly he was overjoyed. The man was a fool and it had taken very little to goad him into this uncouth behaviour.

'So you are your fiancée's landlord?' Godfrey enquired.

'That's right. And right now I feel your presence here is an intrusion.'

Inwardly, Godfrey was elated. All it would take would be one little nudge to push this buffoon over the edge.

'My presence here is warranted,' he said, 'because I have paid to Mr Micawber a substantial contribution towards the rent.'

Ridger stood up, his face red with anger. 'And Mr Larkfield informs me that arrears are still outstanding.'

Emma burst into tears, clutching her head in her hands.

'Stop that ridiculous bawling,' Ridger shouted. 'I'll have a word with my father about this – this' – he pointed at Godfrey – 'this new tenant. Unless we have some of the arrears paid, we may have to evict him.'

Ridger swept out of the room and slammed the front door so hard the timbers shook. He squinted from the glare of the angry sun as he untethered his horse from the post, and glowered as he looked back at the open parlour window from where he had heard Emma playing the piano on his arrival. Playing the piano! For him! And when she had opened the front door, the flustered expression and the guilty look in her eyes, which he had interpreted as embarrassment following their quarrel, he now suspected was because he had caught her on intimate terms with McNeil. And why did she have to belittle him in front of the lodger? Repeating that remark he had made about the story needing more action, almost as if she deliberately wanted to humiliate him in front of the other man. Not only that, but she seemed less supportive of him than that damned McNeil. And the sly glances she had made in the lodger's direction hadn't gone unnoticed either.

As he climbed on to his horse and wheeled it around, tugging the rein roughly, he began to fantasize about married life with Emma. He would show her who was boss. A woman wasn't going to get the better of him, he would see to that once they were married and she had legally become his property.

Alarmed at Ridger's unnecessary outburst, Emma had shot to her feet as he walked out, dabbing her eyes with a handkerchief. Godfrey rose slowly in the heavy silence and they stared at one another, both communicating what they knew to be the truth about Emma's fiancé. He was uncivilized and uncultured and nothing was going to change that.

Eventually, Emma broke eye contact and walked to the piano, standing with her back to Godfrey.

'I'm sorry,' she mumbled. 'His behaviour was inexcusable, but I suppose it was understandable, in the circumstances.'

'Yes, you are probably right. His behaviour was perfectly understandable. He must have noticed the intimacy in our relationship, which is why he flew into a jealous rage.'

Emma spun round to confront Godfrey. 'Intimacy! Don't flatter yourself, Mr McNeil. You are a friend of my brother who has come to live here as a lodger. Nothing more.'

Godfrey took a step nearer to her. 'Oh, Emma, please don't try to deny your true feelings. Ever since I first saw you I felt as if my life had changed forever, and I have been thinking of you every single moment of—'

'Stop it!' Emma cried. 'I am engaged to marry Mr Ridger Begs. His behaviour just now was not typical. He is a very sensitive soul.'

'And I am guessing that the awkwardness you both felt was to do with a quarrel you had. Am I right?'

Emma refused to answer and stared at the floor.

'Yes, I thought so. Mr Begs looked to me the sort of person who could make your life a misery when you are married. You are intellectually superior to him and he knows that and resents it.'

Emma raised her eyes and made eye contact with Godfrey again.

'I'm right, aren't I?' he said.

'He has some admirable qualities, Godfrey.'

Godfrey laughed harshly. 'Hah! From what I saw, the man is an uncouth, boorish oaf. And you know in your heart of hearts that I speak the truth.'

Godfrey moved forward a pace and Emma squeezed back against the piano.

'Nevertheless, I am his fiancée and I will stick by him.'

Godfrey paused while he regarded her gravely. He waited until he had her full attention before speaking. 'I know why you're doing this, agreeing to a marriage that is a mismatch in every sense of the word.'

'Oh, and why is that?'

'You're doing it for your family. Once you are married to that clown, perhaps Mr Begs will find employment for his father-in-law and all will be well. He won't want his son's in-laws to suffer from penury and bring disgrace to the family, a family who are fast becoming one of the most influential in Melbourne.'

Emma, her face flushed, raised her voice. 'If you think this will be a marriage of convenience—'

But Godfrey wouldn't let her finish. 'Please, Emma! I urge you not to do it. Consider your own feelings. Forgive me: I was wrong to suggest you are marrying him for reasons of security. But perhaps you have allowed yourself to be swept along and are now finding it difficult to back down. Listen to me, Emma: you have your whole life to consider. Please, don't throw it away.'

He stepped forward and gently took her hand. 'I love you, Emma. I can't let you marry him. Fate has driven us together and love will bind us forever.'

For a moment Emma was confused, struggling with her feelings towards him and terrified of his words. Then she recovered, snatched her hand away, and dashed from the room, saying, 'Please! Leave me alone, Godfrey. Leave me alone.'

Godfrey smiled as he watched her fleeing from the room. He knew by her feeble protests that she would very soon be his, and her ridiculous fiancé would be but a disagreeable memory.

28

Wilkins Micawber, Detective

EARLY THE FOLLOWING morning, while Emma took the twins to school, accompanied by Godfrey, Micawber sat in the parlour studying his advertisement in the *Melbourne Chronicle* again, and wondered if it would prove to be fruitful. His wife entered and placed a cup of tea on an occasional table close to his chair. She stood over him, frowning deeply, and he asked if something was troubling her.

'Yes, Wilkins,' she replied. 'I am worried about Emma and young Godfrey McNeil. They seem to be – how shall I describe it?' She glanced at the piano. 'Harmonious is the word that springs into my mind.'

Mirroring his wife's frown, Micawber said, 'I take your meaning, My Dear. At our fine repast last night, I couldn't help but notice the way their sidelong glances met, and how Godfrey sparkled with wit and erudition, as if he was playing a tune and she was his instrument.'

'Yes,' Mrs Micawber acknowledged. 'And *I* couldn't help but notice how she laughed and hung on his every word.'

Suddenly, Mrs Micawber scurried over to her *chaise-longue*, sat on the edge of the seat and commenced wringing her hands.

'Oh, Wilkins!' she cried. 'What's to become of us?'

'Us?' Micawber questioned, the worried frown changing to one of puzzlement.

'Yes, Emma's wagon was firmly hitched to young Ridger Begs's

183

star. And the future seemed bright until recently. I know it may seem a trifle inconsiderate, but if their relationship should wither on the vine, it will surely affect the entire Micawber family. Except Wilkins Junior, of course, who is now a celebrated performer.'

'A separation of the engaged couple would most certainly create untold problems for us. To begin with, we would no longer have the support of Begs Senior, who would undoubtedly sever cordial associations with the Micawbers and revert to pragmatic interests. In short, he would want his rent paid promptly. But we mustn't allow our sentiments to wallow in self-interest. We have Emma's feelings to consider. Even before the bright young Godfrey made an appearance, I had noticed the young Begs was somewhat lacking in cerebral aspirations and quested for more corporeal pursuits which seemed better suited to his benighted disposition. In short, the man is a dunderhead.'

'Wilkins!'

'It has to be said.'

Mrs Micawber had a pinched, shocked look on her face, thoughts tumbling around in her head like paper in a gale.

'But Wilkins,' she croaked, her heart sinking by the minute, 'we are flummoxed once more. What is to become of us?'

Micawber searched for an answer with which to satisfy his dearest, his eyes darting about the room as he sought inspiration. They settled on the newspaper on his lap. The advertisement! Of course! It was just possible that someone might need his services as an inquiry agent.

He tapped the paper with an optimistic index finger. 'This may well be our liberator.'

'Wilkins, I very much doubt that detection will be the answer we so—' Mrs Micawber began, but was interrupted by a soft tapping on the front door.

Micawber sat bolt upright. The person knocking was not using their code, but the creditors had been given money on account, and the gentle knock was timid rather than aggressive. Micawber felt hopeful.

'My Dear, I can feel it in my bones: the knock is reassuring. And I would hazard a guess that it is not serendipitous, but has come about as a result of this timely advertisement; and as I mentioned the advertisement only moments ago, then perhaps the knock is synchronous.'

Micawber rose. 'Please don't get up, My Angel. I will answer it.'

While he went out to the hall to open the front door, his wife tiptoed to the parlour door, which he had left ajar, and listened.

The girl who stood on their veranda couldn't have been more than sixteen, wearing a blue bonnet with blonde ringlets poking from beneath. She had delicate features, a snub nose, and was pale and attractive, as though she was made from bone china.

'Are you the detective?' she asked.

Micawber's heart leapt with excitement. He nodded furiously. 'It is I, the very same, Wilkins Micawber, Detective, at your service.'

She handed him a letter. 'My mistress, Mrs Beatrice de Mornay, would like to see you at three o'clock this afternoon.'

She turned to go.

'One moment,' Micawber said. 'Where does your mistress live?'

'It's in the letter,' said the girl, and she hurried away, raising her skirt slightly with both hands to keep it from trailing in the dirt.

Mr Micawber watched her scurrying with head bowed, avoiding unwelcome attention, until she was out of sight, and then closed the door and returned to the parlour. Smiling, he waved the letter in front of his wife.

'This may be the answer to our prayers.'

'Open it!' she said, unable to conceal her excitement.

Beaming, Micawber slit open the envelope and withdrew a single sheet of paper. Mrs Micawber came and stood at his side and peered over his shoulder.

The letter was written in fine copperplate in bright blue ink.

Silver Beeches
Kingston Road
St Kilda
Melbourne

Dear Sir
I saw your advertisement offering your services as a detective and I
would be grateful if you would call to see me at three o'clock today
to discuss a matter of some stolen property.
Yours faithfully
Beatrice de Mornay (Mrs)

Mrs Micawber sucked in air excitedly. 'Silver Beeches at St Kilda, Wilkins. I am sure that was the impressive mansion we saw when we went walking yesterday. High up on the hill with a splendid view of the ocean.'

'I think you may be right, My Angel.'

'But if this woman has had something stolen, how will you know where to look for it?'

'That, My Dearest, remains to be seen. Until I meet with Mrs de Mornay I am entirely in the dark. But first things first. We still have a little of the money left that Godfrey gave us, do we not?'

'We have a small sum set aside to pacify Mr Larkfield.'

Micawber drew to his full height and waved the letter in the air. 'That can wait. For I have now obtained a paid commission to solve a mystery of some stolen property. And just as our new Victoria Police Force is easily recognized in a distinctive uniform, I too must go in search of suitable attire for the position of detective.'

'But you are being hired as a private inquiry agent, and I take private to mean strictly confidential. If you start running about in a uniform—'

Micawber sighed with impatience. 'I am not suggesting

purchasing a uniform. My intention is to wear garments that are appropriate to the occupation of detective, however private that might be, in order to inspire confidence in my first client.'

Micawber stared at his wife, challenging her to contradict his motive. She smiled and clapped her hands.

'Oh, Wilkins! Your first case as a detective. How thrilling.' Her smile suddenly faded. 'But what if you discover the stolen property is in the hands of a vicious ruffian?'

He hadn't considered this possibility, and began to look worried. 'I cannot perceive what destiny may hold. That is beyond the realms of attainability, so I will render my mind free from the preoccupations of dangers that may lurk ahead. In short, I will cross that bridge when I come to it.'

29

A Mystery Solved

MICAWBER LOOKED UP at the impressive Silver Beeches and began to climb the steps leading up to it. By the time he reached the mansion's gate at the top, he was puffed. He removed his battered top hat and mopped his brow. His heart beat fast and his temperature soared, which may have been as much to do with the stressful notion of dealing with a violent thief as the weather. And the cloak he wore was stifling, but its purchase he felt was a masterful touch, giving him the appearance of a detective. Although, coupled with the top hat, he looked as if he was on his way to the opera.

He replaced his hat and tried the heavy wrought-iron gate. It was locked and he could see there was no bell or any way of making his presence known. He was a little early, and perhaps they would send someone to meet him at three o'clock.

He turned and looked back at the picturesque scene below. Young couples and children strolled along the esplanade that ran along the beach, and colourful and moveable bathing huts were dotted here and there in the sand. Anchored at sea were dozens of ships and everything had the illusion of stillness, as if this was a giant painting.

'Excuse me, sir!'

Micawber started. He hadn't heard anyone approaching and he spun round. It was the young maid who had visited them early that morning. She was now dressed in black with a white pinafore.

'My mistress is expecting you,' she said, sliding an enormous key into the lock. The gate squeaked open and Micawber entered. When she had closed and locked the gate, she said, 'Follow me, please,' and led the way up more steps towards the mansion's entrance.

As he followed, Micawber began thinking as a detective ought to think, even though he hadn't been instructed yet about the crime. Obviously the security at the house was satisfactory, and presumably there were other servants, not just this maid. And he had noticed the wall surrounding the house must have been at least six feet high and was protected by broken glass set into the concrete at the top. Because the mansion was raised even higher up the hill, the wall did not mask the view of this fine building with its impressive colonial-style pillars.

The front garden was layered in a series of terraces, alternating between lawn and beds of flowers and shrubs. By the time they reached the massive front door, Micawber was wheezing from the effort of the climb. The maid regarded him with suspicion, as if she wondered what a middle-aged, unfit man was doing chasing after a thief.

'This way,' she said, pushing open the door. 'And to your left, please.'

He just had time to glimpse an enormous chandelier below a curving marble staircase, and the black and white chequered floor, before he was ushered into a drawing room that was predominantly green. As he entered he removed his hat and came face to face with his hostess, standing with her back to a marble fireplace, waiting to greet him.

'Mr Micawber,' she said. 'Do come in.'

She was younger than he had expected. She couldn't have been more than twenty-six or seven, with an attractive rounded face, dark olive skin and large brown eyes, and her long jet hair flowed to the middle of her back. As she regarded Micawber, she didn't smile, and looked him up and down, evaluating his worth as a claimant to the title of detective.

'You advertised your services as a detective?' she questioned, as if she couldn't quite believe it.

Micawber nodded his assent. 'That is correct.'

'And what experience do you have?'

Micawber paused. This was a tricky question but one for which he was prepared. He tapped the side of his head with an index finger. 'I have experience of solving problems. You may have heard of the Great Jupiter who recently performed at the Queen's Theatre. The audience marvelled at his illusions and were overwhelmed and baffled, and left the theatre wondering how he managed his deceptions. I, on the other hand, disentangled the skeins of his mysteries. If you have a problem, a mystery to solve, then I, Wilkins Micawber, will discover clues, eliminate suspects, and arrive at a solution. Of course, until such time as I am apprised of the crime, I remain in a condition of ignorance.'

The maid, standing to the left of Micawber, stared at him openmouthed. She had never before encountered such a rare specimen and wondered if all detectives behaved in this strange fashion. Her mistress, on the other hand, regarded him with a trace of amusement and gestured to a chair.

'Please, Mr Micawber, sit down. You must be thirsty after the climb up here. May I offer you a glass of lemonade?'

As he sank into the comfortable chair, Micawber thanked her. She nodded to her maid, who walked to a small table on which stood glasses and a jug of lemonade, poured a glass and handed it to him.

'Thank you, Betty, you may go now,' Mrs de Mornay said.

After the maid had gone, Mrs de Mornay sat in a chair facing Micawber.

'This is a very puzzling theft, indeed,' she said. 'But let me start at the beginning. My husband and I emigrated from the north of England more than three months ago, but – for reasons I needn't bother to explain – some of our more precious family heirlooms were forwarded only a few weeks ago. They came on the SS *Great Britain* and made the journey in only ninety days.'

Micawber sipped his lemonade and said, 'The speed of our transport now is remarkable. Remarkable.'

Mrs De Mornay seemed irritated by his interruption and her lip twitched before she continued, 'We had many crates and packing cases, and each one was sealed and numbered with a list of what each one contained. I had begun unpacking some of the cases, assisted by my maid Betty, and I wanted to supervise the entire process of the task, to make absolutely certain nothing was damaged during the journey.

'My husband, incidentally, is Sir Richard de Mornay, and he is in Sydney on business for a month and will be returning any day now.'

Micawber nodded enthusiastically, looking suitably impressed.

Mrs de Mornay continued, 'We employ Betty, whom you have met, of course, and we also have a gardener, a coachman – who has driven my husband to Sydney – a cook and a housemaid. We do not have a family yet, so we find our staff sufficient for our needs. Unfortunately, three weeks ago our gardener became severely ill, and an opportunity presented itself when my housemaid met a young man who was looking for sporadic employment. She mentioned him to me and I asked to meet him. He was Irish, and he seemed a charming enough man. He worked for me for three days, and I paid him on a daily basis. On the fourth day he didn't arrive for work, and I didn't give it another thought, thinking he had probably gone to try his luck prospecting for gold. But then I noticed that one of my husband's family heirlooms was missing, and one that is of great sentimental value to him. If it was this young Irishman who stole it, it is most puzzling, since he could so easily have taken other items of value. I have many items of jewellery, which could have been concealed far easier than the item he may have stolen. I would so much like to find this article, as it has been in my husband's family for generations.'

'Perhaps,' Micawber said, 'you could describe this article for me.'

While Mrs de Mornay went on to describe the stolen object, Micawber took a sip of the refreshing drink, which was not overly sweet or tart.

'The missing object is a crystal wine decanter, Mr Micawber, and it is decorated with a distinctive fleur-de-lis.'

Micawber coughed and spluttered, his eyes watered and the lemonade went up his nose. He tried to compose himself and dabbed his eyes with a corner of his cloak.

Mrs de Mornay, a mixed expression of concern and irritation leant forward. 'Are you all right, Mr Micawber?'

Micawber's voice croaked as he tried to recover. 'I swallowed rather too suddenly.'

'Is something wrong? You look as if you have just seen hounds from Hades.'

'No, no, I am blooming.' He cleared his throat as delicately as possible and punctuated the air with an index finger. 'I am robust and vigorous and ready to solve the mystery of your missing decanter.'

Mrs de Mornay peered at him through narrowed lids. 'Hmm. You certainly look a long way from robust if you don't mind my observing.'

Micawber smiled weakly.

'Now, would you mind telling me how you propose to recover our property?'

Micawber struggled to remain calm and his mind raced ahead. The de Mornay decanter stood on his sideboard, and he would be able to retrieve the object and return it to its owners within an instant. But he could hardly tell her the truth, otherwise she might summon the Victoria Police, and Godfrey could end up behind bars. For Micawber was under no illusion that Godfrey had stolen the item.

'First of all,' Micawber said, 'I will try to eliminate all your servants from my inquiry.'

Mrs de Mornay clicked her tongue impatiently. 'My servants are extremely honest and reliable. You have met Betty. Does she strike you as a young girl who would steal a decanter? And you can eliminate our coachman who is in Sydney. Around the time the decanter disappeared our cook was shopping with the assistance of the housemaid. No, I am convinced it was the young Irishman, who vanished hastily and was never seen again, even though there was plenty of work for him had he chosen to return.'

'Can you describe this Irishman to me?'

Mrs de Mornay tilted her head and thought about it for a moment before speaking. 'His face was quite pleasant but rather ordinary. There was nothing extravagantly memorable about it. He was perhaps in his middle twenties and had fairly long auburn hair.'

'Curly?' Micawber enquired.

'Yes. But how can you possibly know that?'

'Er – I don't. I'm just examining every possibility.'

He was relieved to see his hostess seemed satisfied with this answer.

'Do you think, judging by what I have told you, you might track him down?'

Micawber shook his head and turned his palms up in a gesture of helplessness. 'It seems unlikely.'

'Then how do you plan to recover my decanter?'

'There are various ways. It is doubtful the miscreant still has the item, and will either have pawned or sold it. I will start with the pawnbrokers, and if that is a hollow quest, then I will make inquiries in Canvas Town. The decanter you have described is distinctive.'

'But even if, as you suggest, the thief has sold our decanter, the present owner of the item would be reluctant to part with it.'

'Ah, that would be a complication.'

Mrs de Mornay turned and paced several times, frowning

thoughtfully, before facing Micawber again. 'Why don't you let it be known that you are offering a five pound reward for the decanter? I will give you the money, which is perhaps more than the object is worth – except to my husband. Now tell me, Mr Micawber, what do you charge for your investigations?'

Micawber coughed discreetly. 'Ahem! I charge two pounds per day, and if I am successful—'

Mrs de Mornay waved it aside. 'I will pay you fifteen pounds if you are successful. I will advance you five pounds for your trouble, with the five pounds reward for finding it, and if you should succeed in finding the decanter and returning it to me, I will pay you the outstanding ten pounds. How does that sound?'

Micawber opened and closed his mouth like a fish. 'Thank you. It is most generous.'

'It is much more than the decanter is worth, but for sentimental reasons I would like it back in our family.'

'I will do everything in my power to find it.'

Mrs de Mornay stared into the distance, and she echoed her thoughts aloud. 'I cannot help thinking that the young Irishman – for I am sure it was he who stole the decanter – was not motivated by money or greed, but by some other design; otherwise he would have taken far more precious items of jewellery.'

Micawber's thoughts ran along the same lines, and he couldn't fathom why on earth Godfrey would risk stealing a decanter and then present it as a gift to the Micawber family. The young man's conduct was hard to comprehend.

It was as Micawber hurried along the St Kilda esplanade that the answer came to him. He had pushed thoughts of Godfrey's motive in giving them the decanter to the back of his mind, but now the reason the young man wanted to ingratiate himself with the Micawber family seemed obvious. It should have been apparent from the start. He had fallen for Emma and wanted to court her.

As he pounded along, deep in thought, his heart beat out a rhythm that he found exhilarating. He was a detective and he had solved the mystery of the woman's missing decanter. Now all he had to do was return it to her and collect the reward.

But if his beating heart and steps were well co-ordinated, his mind became a jumble of mixed emotions. He had been given two beautiful five pound notes and one of them was to pay a non-existent person a reward for surrendering the stolen object; but Micawber owned the decanter and would now be forced to act dishonestly, keep the extra five pounds, and make up a story about its repossession.

Alternatively, he could act truthfully, explain to Mrs de Mornay what had happened, and hope she wouldn't inform the police. That was a grave risk to take, because once she had learnt the truth there would be no going back. And if he made up a convincing story about how he performed an act of derring-do to procure the stolen article, she would be impressed and this might reflect upon his future employment as a detective.

But would he be able to accept the entire twenty pounds for having done nothing deserving? And it made him feel wretched to think that his work in solving the crime was bogus. It remained to be seen whether or not he was capable of actually solving a mystery other than diversions such as riddles.

And then there was the problem of Godfrey McNeil, who had presumably resorted to theft because he was in love. He had resisted any temptation to steal items of real value, and probably stole the decanter because it was in a crate, waiting to be unpacked, and thought it wouldn't be missed.

But a theft was still a theft and a thief was still a thief, and Micawber began to wonder about Godfrey's background. Young Wilkins had introduced him into the family over two months ago, but he had never spoken about his past. What was his history? Where was he from?

As he reached the centre of Melbourne, now dripping in

perspiration, with his damp clothes clinging to his body, Micawber's conflicts deepened. He was confronted by thoughts of how advantageous it was that Emma should remain betrothed to Ridger Begs and that nothing should tear this union asunder. His family would certainly benefit from this union, but if his daughter fell for Godfrey and repudiated young Ridger, then they all stood to suffer.

Perhaps he should inform the police about Godfrey, thus removing him from the potentially damaging threat of an amorous entanglement. On the other hand, to do this could result in Mrs de Mornay finding out.

One of the biggest problems facing Micawber was accepting a full twenty pounds for the bogus detective work. Temptation was being waved in front of him, and he argued himself senseless, telling himself she was a wealthy woman and all she desired was to have her property returned.

Finally, he came to the conclusion that his first plan of action would be to take Godfrey aside, confront him about the theft and shame him into leaving their household.

He felt almost tearful as he neared his home, because he liked Godfrey and preferred him to Ridger. The nearer he drew to their house, the shorter his steps became, and he approached reluctantly at snail's pace. Then, as he walked up the few steps to the veranda, he was suddenly struck by an idea, and he knew exactly what he had to do regarding Godfrey. It would also put his detective skills to the test.

30

Micawber's Trick

AFTER HANGING UP his hat and cloak in the hall, Micawber entered the parlour and found his wife dusting the furniture. She spun round as he entered and her eyes were filled with hope. Although the future was racked with difficulties, he wanted to present her with a positive outlook before she heard the calamitous news, so he took the five pound notes out of his pocket and waved them in front of her.

She gasped with delight. 'Wilkins! Where did you get that money?'

He smiled. 'From Mrs de Mornay.'

'She is employing you as a detective?'

'She most certainly is. But the situation is burdened by a plethora of complications.'

'Complications?'

Mrs Micawber's imagination ran unchecked as she pictured her husband striding into dens of iniquity and confronting hardened criminals over stolen booty, and imagined him being bludgeoned to death by a brutish man with an eye patch, before leaping forward in time to his graveside, where she saw herself tearfully tossing a flower into his grave.

Seeing the look of alarm on his wife's face, Micawber took her hand and said, 'My Dear, we are at a crossroads, and our direction must be determined by our will to plump for the right avenue. Do we forge straight ahead, but risk crossing a busy junction? Or do we select a path that appears to be sensible but may have serious repercussions. In short, we are confronted by choices.'

'Wilkins! I have no idea what you are talking about.'

Micawber gave her a reassuring smile before embarking on his long story. He left nothing out, for he always told his Dear Wife everything. When he had finished, and he had presented her with all the options, she asked him what he intended doing.

'First of all, My Dear,' he began, 'please tell me where Emma and Godfrey are this very minute.'

'Godfrey accompanied our daughter to collect the twins. And you should see how well they are getting on together. I mean, of course, Emma and that young man. She hangs on his every word and laughs at his witticisms. And when he gazes into her eyes he—'

As she now thought of Godfrey as a thief, and one who was a threat to their wellbeing, Mrs Micawber broke off tearfully. She forgot the duster in her hand was not a handkerchief, dabbed her eyes on it and blew her nose.

'Please, My Angel, keep calm,' Micawber said. 'They will be returning soon and I am relying on you to maintain an unflustered demeanour. Godfrey must suspect nothing. Mrs de Mornay described the culprit as Irish, so he may well be an innocent party in this tale of woe. Perhaps he unwittingly purchased the stolen decanter from the miscreant with the intention of presenting it to us as a gift.'

'In order to cultivate a relationship with our daughter,' Mrs Micawber hissed.

Micawber made a steadying gesture with his hand. 'Keep calm. I intend to get at the truth, using skills that a detective employs. As soon as they arrive home, remain perfectly natural while I question Godfrey – perhaps on the veranda outside, free from any interruption.'

They heard the front door opening and looked at one another in alarm.

'Remember,' Micawber whispered, 'everything must remain natural and commonplace.'

Mrs Micawber broke away and began dusting the sideboard just as the twins rushed in, followed by Emma and Godfrey.

'Papa!' Edward cried. 'Emma and Godfrey are going to play cards with us.'

'Yes,' Emily added. 'We're going to play Ranter Go Round.'

Godfrey laughed. 'Although I can't say I'm familiar with that game.'

'It is sometimes called Cuckoo,' Micawber said. 'But before you children get carried away I need a word in private with Godfrey. Perhaps your Mama could make up a foursome for the cards.'

Edward pulled a face. 'Oh, but, Papa ...'

'Do as your father tells you, Edward, there's a good boy,' Mrs Micawber said. 'I will attend to supper in a little while.' She caught her husband's eye. 'I would really enjoy a game of cards.'

Leaving Emma and her mother to play cards with the twins, Micawber took Godfrey outside and made certain they were not close to the open window where they might be overheard. They both squinted in the sun's glare and there was a moment's silence while Godfrey, who felt a tension in his shoulders, plucked up the courage to open the proceedings.

'You said you wished to speak with me privately.'

'It's about my son, Young Wilkins,' Micawber lied. 'I'm worried about him becoming an actor.'

Godfrey let his breath out slowly, relieved that the conversation was not going to be about his relationship with Emma, which was what he had suspected.

'Why should your son's career disturb you? He seems to have discovered his vocation in life.'

'I wouldn't like to see him fail.'

'I don't fully understand your concerns. I am sure Wilkins will make a fine actor.'

'Yes, but I have only ever seen him play one type of role, using his own voice. In order to succeed in the theatre, versatility is a requisite; and I have never, for instance, ever heard Young Wilkins speak with another dialect.'

Feeling completely at ease now, Godfrey laughed confidently. 'Oh, Young Wilkins is very bright. He will soon adapt. He has the ear to learn many dialects, of that I'm certain.'

Micawber shook his head and pushed out his bottom lip. 'Oh, I'm not so sure. For instance, it must require enormous verbal dexterity for an actor to convince his audience that he is a native of Scotland.'

Laughing loudly, Godfrey rattled off a stream of dialogue in a Highlands dialect.

Micawber gave him a little ripple of applause. 'Most impressive,' he said.

'Thank you. But it is not so very difficult. It is something your son can learn to do.'

'Well, I'm not wholly convinced. One swallow, as the saying goes, does not make a summer.'

Godfrey gave an exasperated sigh. 'It really is not so very complicated. Give me another dialect, and I will see if I can do it.'

'Um …' Micawber hesitated, giving the impression he was plucking a dialect randomly out of the air. 'What about … Irish?'

Hardly giving himself time to think about it, Godfrey launched into a speech from an obscure play set in the west of Ireland. He faltered after four sentences and excused the lapse by blaming his memory.

'Yes, I concede that numerous dialects are attainable through keeping one's ears open.' Micawber said, frowning thoughtfully as he stared at an almost identical wooden bungalow opposite, where a mangy dog lay curled asleep on the veranda.

'Is that it, sir?' Godfrey asked after a long pause. 'I appreciate you are concerned about your son but—'

Micawber swung round to face him. 'I expect you are wondering why I wanted our discussion in private.'

'That had crossed my mind, sir.'

'It is because of this: today, in my first commission as a private inquiry agent, a lady asked me to retrieve a stolen object. The lady's name is Mrs de Mornay and the object in question is a glass decanter with a fleur-de-lis.'

Micawber studied Godfrey's reaction carefully, but the young man's face was a blank canvas.

'Now the lady described to me the young man who was employed by her to do some gardening, and you appear to fit that description, Godfrey. She also said the thief was Irish, and you have just demonstrated to me that you are perfectly capable of impersonating an Irishman. So please do not insult my intelligence by telling me that you are not that same person who made off with her property – property that is of sentimental value to her husband. Well, what have you go to say for yourself?'

Godfrey's eyes became moist and there was a rasp in his voice. 'I would never insult your intelligence, Mr Micawber. I can only say how deeply sorry I am. I cannot excuse my actions. The theft was a stupid impulse which I now regret.'

Micawber regarded him through narrowed eyes. 'That cannot be true, for when Mrs de Mornay employed you as a gardener, you passed yourself off as an Irishman, and therefore you must have been intending a deception of some sort.'

'I cannot carry on with this duplicity a moment longer. I will tell you everything, sir.'

Godfrey had a sad, faraway look in his eyes, and lowered his voice so that Micawber had to strain to hear his confession.

'Your son, Wilkins, almost guessed about my past from something I let slip when I coached him in his Hamlet speech. I grew up in London, in a reasonable neighbourhood in Islington. My father was very like you, Mr Micawber – passionately fond of books and the arts, and worked as a librarian. My mother was a nurse and I had quite a happy childhood. I wanted to be an actor and I was encouraged by my father. But tragedy struck when I was only fourteen. Setting off for work one morning, my father stepped out into the road without looking and was killed by a brewery dray. My mother never got over the loss and she died just over a year later from a brain disease, although I suspect it was a broken heart. I went to live with her older brother, but he was intolerant of my ambitions, and I left to make my own way in the world as an actor. I don't need to describe the hardships of those early years, where I spent most of every waking hour fetching, carrying, mending costumes, and painting scenery. Eventually, after many years serving this apprenticeship, I began playing some leading roles in small theatre companies. Times were still very hard but I survived until five years ago when I was employed by an actor/manager who was a scoundrel. After many false promises of payment, he decamped with the box office takings leaving the cast high and dry.

'I was destitute, with not a farthing to my name, and for the first time in my life I stole something. It was only a meat pie. I know that is no excuse, but I was starving hungry. I was caught in the act of stealing, tried and given seven years' hard labour, and transported to Van Diemen's Land. Less than two years later I and two other convicts escaped in a fishing boat across the Bass Strait, and we managed to hide in Melbourne. So you see, the police will have details of our escape. We are wanted men, still on the run; and, as neither of the other two convicts was Irish, I thought by pretending to be Irish, I wouldn't arouse Mrs de Mornay's suspicions.'

When Godfrey had finished speaking, Micawber sighed deeply and shook his head, thinking about all that had been said.

'I don't want to go back to Van Diemen's Land. I know transportation there has ended but I still owe the government a few more years of my life. I would sooner die than return to that terrible island where the cruelty is unbelievable; where settlers hunt and kill the natives mercilessly like wild animals.'

Micawber chewed his lip thoughtfully, while Godfrey waited for him to make a pronouncement.

'The theft of the meat pie is a forgivable transgression, and the inhuman retribution was inappropriate. However, when a superficial object is appropriated—'

'Forgive me for interrupting, sir, for I can guess what you are about to say. I did a terrible wrong in stealing that decanter, but I thought it was an item that had little value and would not be missed. I was wrong. And stealing a functional ornament was an act of desperation.'

Micawber turned his hands palms over. 'For once I am at a loss.'

'I was lonely, terribly lonely, and always fearful of the law catching up with me; and then I struck up a friendship with your son and he introduced me into your family. I sought acceptance by you and your family, sir, and wanted to bring you a decorous gift.'

'And would this Trojan horse have anything to do with courting my daughter?'

Godfrey became flustered and started gabbling. 'No, no, Mr Micawber, it wasn't like that. I loved being welcomed into your family. I miss my own family, although I was an only son: two of my siblings were stillborn. And you, sir, are not unlike my own father, who was a man of intellect and sensitivity.'

Micawber stared out over the veranda and rubbed his chin. 'I am at a loss. A faultless decision is unachievable. Wise men do judge, and honest men do pity. Forgive my descent into sententiousness, but I am well and truly floored!'

'You won't inform the police about my escape, will you?' Godfrey asked, his voice shaky.

'I find myself incapable of such an unmerciful deed.'

Godfrey took Micawber's hand and shook it exuberantly. 'Thank you, sir. It was the thing I most dreaded. I don't know how I can ever repay you for such an act of kindness.'

'Perhaps you can repay me by leaving our house.'

Their hands broke apart, and the pleading in Godfrey's eyes made Micawber think of a cruelly treated dog.

'One week, I beg you. Just one week and I will be gone from Melbourne.'

'Where will you go?'

Godfrey merely shrugged. Micawber began to feel sympathetic towards him, and a little bit ashamed of the way he had bluntly asked him to leave their house.

'On the other hand, you have advanced a share of the rent that extends to another *two* weeks. So why not spend that time with us making arrangements for your future?'

Tears sprang into Godfrey's eyes. Micawber looked away in embarrassment and changed the subject.

'Now, about the decanter, which I am instructed to detect and return....'

Godfrey hung his head shamefully. 'Yes, I gave you a present, and now you must give it back. How could I think of doing such a despicable deed?' He raised his head and a glint came into his eye. 'Would you mind me asking, sir, how much the lady is prepared to pay for its return?'

'She gave me five pounds as a reward to ferret out a receiver of the stolen item, five pounds as a retainer for my services, and will pay another ten pounds for its recovery.'

Godfrey gave a low whistle. 'Well, all you have to do is wait a day or two, to give credibility to your search, return the decanter – making up a story about how you found it – and you are twenty pounds richer.'

'I will, however, struggle with my conscience.'

'But the lady is extremely wealthy.'

'Their house certainly seemed palatial.'

'Have you not heard of her husband, Sir Richard de Mornay?' Micawber shook his head. 'He is one of Melbourne's wealthiest men. Look out over the ocean and most of the ships you will see belong to him. He has dozens of merchant ships and passenger vessels, most of which he built in his shipyards in Britain. Twenty pounds to a man like Sir Richard de Mornay is a trifle. Whereas to you, sir – and I am only guessing at the calculation – it is enough to keep the roof over your family's head for a good three months.'

Micawber waved his hands in surrender. 'Dash it all! That prick to my conscience is from the tiniest pin.'

Godfrey laughed heartily. 'And I have just had another bright thought. When you return Sir Richard de Mornay's decanter, you can ask his wife to recommend you as a detective. Considering how influential they are, you will soon be the most eminent detective in all of Australia!'

'I had already considered that aspect of the development.' Micawber smiled, and pictured himself being applauded by rows of uniformed policeman while he stood on a podium and lectured them about detection.

'And that was a brilliant piece of detection the way you tricked me into performing with an Irish dialect.'

Micawber was pleased with the compliment, but also just a little bit suspicious of the easy flattery. He moved awkwardly from one foot to another, and then he suddenly remembered the ten pounds and tapped his breast pocket.

'Something is burning a hole in this pocket. I think I need to purchase wine to go with tonight's supper.'

'Perhaps I could accompany you to the shop, Mr Micawber?'

'Your company is always most welcome, Godfrey.'

Micawber's shoulder was patted in rather an over familiar way by Godfrey, planting a small seed of doubt in his brain. The young man seemed to have regained his confidence with remarkable ease, considering he had been exposed as a thief, not out of necessity but in order to ingratiate himself with the Micawber family.

As they walked along the street, Micawber listening to

Godfrey's future plans, he comforted himself with the thought that two weeks would pass rapidly and then Godfrey would be gone, which was probably a satisfactory outcome in the circumstances.

31

The Letter

EVEN THOUGH GODFREY had been given a two-week sanction to remain in the Micawber household, it took him only two days to change their lives irreparably. Following his confession to Micawber, and a hearty supper, the twins were sent to bed, and Godfrey insisted on telling them a goodnight story. They liked the young man and he was very good with children and seemed to fit in to family life with such a lack of reserve that Micawber felt he would regret his departure.

After returning to the parlour, Godfrey had informed the three of them that he had something to say, and repeated everything he had told Micawber, telling them how stupid he had been, and he had stolen out of a misguided desperation to experience family life once more. His remorse seemed so genuine that none of them doubted his sincerity, and now they knew his history they relaxed in his company.

The next day, Emma took the twins to school as usual, accompanied by Godfrey, and the two of them didn't return until the afternoon, much to the consternation of her father and mother. They had enjoyed a seaside walk at St Kilda, they said, and Micawber and his wife thought no more about it, especially as they had returned in time to fetch Emily and Edward. That evening, everyone was in high spirits, and Godfrey played games with the twins until it was time for bed.

On the second day, Micawber took the decanter back to Mrs

de Mornay, who was so delighted by this result that she promised she would sing his praises at every opportunity, which went some way to ease Micawber's nagging conscience, and the final money transaction also helped to restore a sense of equilibrium.

That evening they celebrated in style, toasting the absent Wilkins Micawber, Junior with an excellent punch mixed by his father, and dined lavishly on beef with all the trimmings, followed by Mrs Micawber's outstanding sherry trifle. Games were played, laughter rang out, and conversation soared to high levels of intellect and humour. Micawber joked that Christmas seemed to have arrived two weeks early. But like all highs, when they are so sweet and sublime, the crash when it happens is devastatingly worse than when things are muddling along in a desultory fashion.

On the morning of the third day the twins awoke to find Emma's bed empty. Their parents, bleary-eyed from the previous night, and suspicious of where their daughter had slept, banged loudly on Godfrey's door. There was no reply, so Micawber threw open the door and found Godfrey's room unoccupied.

They hurried into the parlour, thinking their daughter and Godfrey had risen very early and perhaps they were conversing in the main room. That was when Mrs Micawber's eyes focused on the envelope propped against her Dear Mama's clock. Her heart almost stopped, because she suspected the worst. And she was right. She tore open the letter and began to read, her eyes brimming with tears.

'What does it say?' Micawber asked, his voice a gloomy monotone.

Sobbing, Mrs Micawber read aloud from the letter. '"My Dear Mama and Papa, I hope you will find it in your heart to forgive me. I have fallen in love with Godfrey. I knew from the moment I first met him that he is a finer man than Ridger, whom I could never marry. Because Godfrey is a wanted man, we have decided to escape together to New Zealand and by the time you read this letter our ship will have sailed, so it is no use trying to stop us. Please, please forgive us, and give Edward and Emily a big hug for me".'

She stopped reading as a great tear dripped onto the letter and her shoulders shook. Micawber squeezed her hand.

'Please continue, My Darling.'

Like a dog shaking off water, Mrs Micawber shivered, and carried on reading in a broken voice. '"Hopefully, the authorities may eventually (now that transportation has ended) give up searching for Godfrey – whose real name is Arthur Welbeck – and we may return to Melbourne and I can see my loving family again. Once we are in New Zealand and have found accommodation I will write to you. I love my family so much, and so does Godfrey, and he hopes you will find it in your heart to forgive him. He will, I know, make a worthy son-in-law for you, my dear Mama and Papa, and a wonderful brother-in-law to Young Wilkins, Edward and Emily. Your loving daughter, Emma."'

Mrs Micawber turned with an animal moan and confronted her husband. 'She has eloped, Wilkins!' she wailed. 'Our baby has eloped! It is my fault for trying to push her into the arms of Ridger Begs, and now look what has happened.'

Micawber, his face rigid with pain, muttered, 'You mustn't blame yourself, My Dearest.'

'Our lives have changed. Nothing will ever be the same again.'

Emily and Edward stared at their parents, their expressions grim.

'Why has Emma gone to New Zealand?' Emily asked.

'What does "eloped" mean?' Edward said.

'It means,' their father explained in a trembling voice, 'they have run away to New Zealand to get married.'

'But why can't they get married here?' Emily said. 'I liked Godfrey.'

'So did I,' her brother said.

'It's a bit difficult to explain,' their mother sobbed. 'You see it's impossible for Godfrey to remain in Australia. There are some men after him.'

'Is he an escaped convict?' Edward said. Neither of his parents replied, but he could read the answer in their faces. 'I knew it! I knew it!'

'Hush now, Edward!' his father said. 'You mustn't ever tell anyone. He will soon be related to the Micawber family, and no one must ever know about his past. Promise me you won't tell a soul. You must promise.'

Edward nodded.

'Say it. Say you promise.'

Edward gulped. 'I promise.'

After Micawber had also got Emily to solemnly swear to keep Godfrey's past a secret there was a loud knock on the front door, using the family code. They all froze and looked helplessly at one another.

'Who can that be at this time of the morning?' Mrs Micawber whispered. 'And it is someone who knows the secret code.'

Micawber made certain his robe was fastened tightly around him and said, 'The only way for me to know who it is would be to answer the door.'

While he strode out of the parlour, intent on dealing with whomever it was with alacrity, Mrs Micawber clasped the twins to her side. She wondered if the person calling had anything to do with the recent crisis and she and the twins listened closely as Micawber opened the front door.

Micawber's mouth fell open, although he had no reason to be surprised. After all, Ridger Begs was still engaged to his daughter. The young man held a bunch of flowers in one hand and a small box in the other. Micawber felt uncharacteristically brutal, due to the devastating news he had just received, and the honest, handsome look on the young man's face was now defined by Micawber as insipid.

'You're too late,' he said. 'She's gone.'

Thinking that Emma had just popped out somewhere, perhaps taken the twins to school, Ridger's brow furrowed with confusion and he thought about his mother's advice. She had told him to remain calm, polite and apologize for his boorish behaviour the last time he had called round. He stared at the flowers (his mother's idea), wondering what he should do with them if Emma was away for the entire day.

'Er – maybe I could call back later. I must apologize for my uncouth behaviour towards Mr McNeil. What time will Emma be coming home?'

'She won't be coming home.'

'I don't understand.'

'She has left us permanently and gone to New Zealand.'

'New Zealand!' Ridger yelled, his eyes bulging. 'Why the hell did she do that?'

Seeing the shocked look on the young man's face, Micawber struggled to find the right words; but from the desperate look on his face, Ridger guessed what had happened.

'And this Mr McNeil: where is he?'

Micawber looked down at the floor and mumbled, 'New Zealand.'

When he looked up and saw Ridger's face crumple, Micawber felt sorry for him. In spite of all his masculine pursuits, and physical prowess, he was still an immature child.

'I am most truly sorry,' Micawber said, and saw an instant transformation as Ridger's expression changed from pain to hatred. He swore several times and wished the entire Micawber family to hell, turned around and strode off, hurling the flowers on to the ground behind him.

Micawber went back indoors and asked his wife if she had heard his exchange with Ridger. Shocked by the young man's vicious oaths, Mrs Micawber's face was burning red as she clasped the twins tighter.

'I heard,' she said. 'And I have to tell you this, Wilkins: I never liked that young man. I established a level of tolerance to deal with him but I always felt uncomfortable in his company. Perhaps Emma has made the right choice.'

32

Men of Adventure

LYING ON HIS back in the open police wagon, Ridger opened his eyes and saw myriad stars in a deep black sky. He had no idea where he was, although he could tell by the squeaking springs and the bouncing that he was in some sort of cart. His cheek throbbed, he could swear his nose was broken and he shook with feverish pain. The last thing he remembered was the fight outside the grog shop, but that had been in broad daylight. Now it was late at night and he couldn't tell how the last five or six hours had been spent. His mouth was as dry as old leather, and when he rolled his tongue around he found a gap and discovered he was also missing a tooth. He groaned loudly.

From the front of the wagon he heard a chuckle, and a voice said, 'I think he's coming round.'

The wagon shuddered to a halt and he heard footsteps crunching on gravel. Then two sets of arms pulled him into a sitting position and he was staring into the faces of two policemen.

'Who are you?' he asked.

One of them laughed harshly, and the other one said, 'Come on, my beauty, you're going to regret this when you look in the mirror tomorrow.'

One either side, they raised his arms on to their shoulders and dragged him towards the house. When one of the policemen knocked, he was surprised to find it was Begs himself who answered the door, and then guessed that he wouldn't want any of the servants to see his son in this state. Begs thanked them and gave them each a ten shilling tip, telling them to have a Christmas drink or two.

'Thank you, sir,' one of them said. 'I hope you have a good Christmas, too.'

Begs doubted that he would, not with his drunken, ne'er-do-well son and the Micawber family for company; he didn't yet know the reason Ridger had drunk himself into a stupor.

He managed to get him into the living room where his mother was waiting, trembling with anxiety. As soon as she saw him she looked away, partly from shame and disgust, and also because she couldn't bear to see how his looks had been altered.

His father threw him into a chair and his head lolled from side to side. As Begs stared at the wreck of his son, reeking from alcohol and sweat, his anger erupted.

'You disgusting pig! Filthy disgusting pig! What the hell do you mean by getting drunk and picking fights outside a grog shop? If it hadn't been for a sergeant in the Victoria Police recognizing you, you might have been beaten to death. You spent the last six hours in a police cell and it was the commissioner who whispered the news to me at the club. You're a disgrace! Can you hear me?'

With great effort Ridger tried to keep his head straight and focus on his father. 'I'm trying to remember,' he slurred.

'Oh, are you! So you don't remember keeping the company of loose women in Cremorne Park? You were seen there in the arms of—'

Begs broke off as he caught his wife's eye, and she looked away.

'I was trying to forget,' Ridger said.

'Trying to forget!' his father shouted, and his wife winced, hoping none of the servants could hear. 'What the hell were you trying to forget?'

'Emma. I was trying to forget Emma Micawber. She's eloped to

New Zealand with McNeil. She's gone. She's out of my life forever.'

Begs exchanged a look with his wife, and then clutched his forehead as he tried to think straight. Now he could understand his son's unruly behaviour, although he didn't condone the way he had disgraced the family.

Tears of self-pity blurred Ridger's vision. 'I loved her,' he wept. 'I truly loved her and she's run off with McNeil. How could she do that to me?'

Begs removed his hand from his brow and said to his wife, 'Perhaps you can get him cleaned up and help him to bed. I've had enough. I wish we had never had anything to do with the Micawber family. I always suspected they would be trouble. I'm going to bed, and we'll talk about this in the morning.'

Mrs Begs tiptoed into her son's bedroom the following morning and found him snoring loudly, making an unhealthy grating noise through his damaged nose. She stroked his forehead tenderly before going downstairs to the dining room. She knew she wouldn't have an appetite for breakfast but she needed a cup of strong, sweet tea.

Her husband sat at the table, staring into the distance, an untouched breakfast of bacon and eggs in front of him. She sat opposite him and poured herself some tea. After a reviving sip, she sighed and spoke quietly to Begs.

'What are you going to do?'

His head jerked up, as if he was coming out of a trance. 'I have given the matter considerable thought. Australia will thrive and prosper on men such as Ridger. Australia needs forthright, honest men of actions and deeds. Not parasites such as the Micawber family with their ridiculous old-world attitudes. We need men of adventure and daring, not artists and actors! Parasites the lot of 'em! The question is: what am I going to do about the Micawbers?'

Mrs Begs's lips tightened maliciously. Her son had been deeply wounded, and her instinct to protect him and seek retribution for the anguish he had suffered spawned an intense hatred of the Micawber family.

'Get rid of them,' she spat. 'They are a menace. I'd like to see those people evicted, and the sooner the better.'

The viciousness that came gushing to the surface both surprised and frightened her; even her husband found the level of her hatred disturbing. But he realized maternal instinct is a powerful force, so without saying a word he nodded his agreement, got up from the table and left to find his rent collector.

33

Mrs Micawber's Bewilderment

IT WAS HARD to dispel the gloom which hung over the Micawber house like a dark thunder cloud, as much as Micawber tried to remain unruffled for the sake of the twins, who kept questioning him about Emma. He played games with them and told stories, but they knew his mind was elsewhere and could sense his deep dissatisfaction with life.

The day after Emma had departed for New Zealand Micawber rose early and made an effort to banish negative thoughts from his mind. Mrs Micawber took the twins to school at their normal time, and had just returned and was sitting with her husband in the parlour, discussing for the umpteenth time their daughter's predicament, when they heard the front door banging open. Micawber started to rise, but the parlour door flew open and he found himself face to face with Larkfield and one of Begs's bailiffs.

'Mr Larkfield! You surprise me barging in like this and disturbing our domestic privacy.'

'And I regret to inform you that time has run out. My employer has given me strict orders that you are to be evicted without delay.'

'This is our downfall!' Micawber wailed. 'Rack and ruin! Armageddon has arrived and we are to be condemned to a life of nomadic existence, wandering the land like the lost tribes of Israel.'

For the life of her, Mrs Micawber could not understand why he was making such a fuss. They still had more than twenty pounds left, which was more than enough to pay off the arrears and pay a two month advance if necessary.

'But, Wilkins, we are left with—' she started to say, but he cut her off with a sudden hand gesture like a bad actor playing Macbeth when he sees Banquo's ghost.

'We are left with nothing but our sense of outrage. Our confidence has been crushed and the Gods wreak havoc on us.'

'But hear me out, Wilkins: we have—'

Again Micawber silenced her with a wail and a gesture. 'Ah! Alas, My Dearest, we have nothing. Do you understand? Nothing!'

Micawber stared at her, clearly trying to convey some sort of secret message. She decided to remain silent and leave him to do the talking.

The bailiff, a bull-necked man with an enormous pot belly, coughed loudly, signalling his impatience. Larkfield took it as his cue to expedite the proceedings.

'Mr Micawber, you will be given one hour to abandon this dwelling. If at such time it is still occupied, Talbot here' – Larkfield gestured towards the bailiff – 'will use force if necessary.'

'I understand,' Micawber said. 'But it allows us barely enough time to gather our personal possessions together.'

'I'm sorry, Mr Micawber, but I'm acting under orders.'

'I know you are, Mr Larkfield. But what about this furniture? We cannot possibly transport these items to who knows where our destination may lie.'

Larkfield tilted his head in the direction of the piano. 'I know that instrument was foolishly sold on credit, therefore it is not yours to sell. I take it the rest of the furniture is yours.'

'Everything. In the bedrooms, the utensils in the kitchen. My Dear Wife's *chaise-longue*.'

Larkfield raised a hand to stop him. 'We are running out of time. When we return in one hour, I will bring a horse and cart, and I will pay you five pounds for the lot.'

Micawber sucked in his cheeks and looked aghast. 'Oh, but it is worth three times—'

'I am not a rich man, Mr Micawber. And that is my best and final offer. Take it or leave it.'

Micawber thrust out his hand and Larkfield shook it. 'Thank you, Mr Larkfield. I bear you no grudge, and I wish you and your lady wife the best of luck for the future.'

Larkfield, feeling awkward and uncomfortable, mumbled his thanks and turned to the bailiff. 'Come on, Talbot, we'll get the horse and cart and the padlocks to secure the property, and we'll be back in one hour.'

After they had both gone, Mrs Micawber stared at her husband, her eyes wide and questioning and her voice shrill. 'Wilkins! I am confused. What have you done? We are to be thrust into the street, destitute and begging, our children in rags, and yet you have over twenty pounds in your pocket – enough to pay our board and keep for many months – so why, may I ask, did you not make Mr Larkfield an offer?'

Micawber gave her a weak smile. 'I should like to submit the hypothesis that, since our daughter spurned her fiancé, our tenancy here is no longer welcome and no amount of capital could secure our future under this roof.'

'Conjecture, Wilkins! Conjecture! You didn't even attempt an offer.'

'I made the assumption on the basis that we owe Mr Begs almost two months arrears, which is why I did not make an offer. Think what might have happened if they had accepted the arrears and then hurled us bag and baggage into the street, we would possess – if my calculations are correct – only six pounds, seventeen shillings and sixpence halfpenny. Think how much worse off we would have been.'

'Wilkins! At this very moment we are not exactly bathing in milk and honey,' Mrs Micawber cried, panic beating in her chest. 'What's to become of us? Oh what's to become of us?'

'In our thirst for adventure, we have travelled to the far corner of this globe, but now the time has come for supplementary decisions, and a modification of our purpose. In short, we must search for fresh fields. And I am of the opinion that we should venture to the further reaches of our world. We will go New Zealand.'

Mrs Micawber's excited intake of breath was loud. 'Wilkins! We will see our Emma again. We will be following in her footsteps not so very long after her departure.' Micawber glanced at the clock. 'Five minutes have passed since we were handed our ultimatum. We must proceed impetuously with a regard for the time.'

'But what about all our personal belongings; how will we transport them?'

'We will ask our neighbour, Benjamin Riley, if we can borrow his cart. He has a secure shed where he can store our belongings until we are set to leave.'

Tears of relief threatened to engulf Mrs Micawber. 'You know, Wilkins, this continent is too immeasurable. I believe New Zealand is not so boundless, and more like our mother country. And so I think New Zealand will be your legitimate sphere of action, Wilkins!'

34

The World Turned Upside Down

THE SAILS BILLOWED and flapped in the wind as the ship rose and fell, and the land gradually became a distant dream. The twins, oblivious to the activity of the ship's crew around them, stared wistfully at the receding land, awed by speed at which such a vast country could so quickly become a distant speck.

Micawber stood leaning against the rail, his arm about Edward, and Mrs Micawber stood at his other side, her arm about Emily, enjoying the cool breeze and the fine spray of salt water that occasionally splashed the side of the vessel, sending the foam cascading up the side.

Micawber, eyes half-closed, basked in the rays of the early morning sun on his face and smiled at their good fortune, the way it had all worked out. Following their decision to leave Australia, they had managed to get most of their personal belongings into the handcart borrowed from their sympathetic neighbour before Mr Larkfield and the bailiff returned. They decided not to worry the twins and to collect them from school at the usual time, and found a room in which to stay the night at a lodging-house near Rourke Street. They wanted to leave Melbourne as quickly as possible, so as not to run up a bill at the lodging-house, and so Micawber trudged round shipping offices to see if he could find a ship that would soon be leaving for New Zealand. That was when the simple belief that his optimism would generate good fortune was thoroughly reinforced.

The merchant vessel on which they were sailing belonged to none other than Sir Richard de Mornay, and the office into which Micawber walked was occupied not only by the influential man himself, in discussion with the ship's captain, but his wife also happened to be visiting, and she introduced the 'detective' to her husband. Micawber told them of his recent misfortune and how he was intent on voyaging to New Zealand, and the grateful shipping magnate offered them a free passage on the merchant ship, sailing early the very next morning.

'It is Divine providence!' Micawber had declaimed to his wife when he returned to the lodging-house. 'The gods are appeased and we are in their favour.'

When the twins were collected from school, they were worried at first that they were no longer going home; but their mother and father's excitement was so infectious they soon forgot their worries and talked about seeing their sister once more.

Staring at the hypnotic waves, Edward's active mind suddenly formed an idea and he turned to his father. 'Papa! You know the world is round. And Great Britain is up here' – he demonstrated with his hands in a circle – 'Australia is on the other side and lower down. And I think New Zealand is lower still. So I think, since leaving England, we have turned upside down. We are upside down.'

Emily giggled and snorted. Micawber smiled happily.

'You are probably right, Edward. We may well be upside down, but we are still upright and on our own two feet.'

Mrs Micawber was aware that he spoke metaphorically and squeezed his arm affectionately. She sighed with contentment.

Emily was frowning at the distant fading land, as if it worried her in some way. 'Mama,' she said, 'what will Papa do in New Zealand? What will his work be?'

'We don't know yet. But I'm sure there will be many opportunities.'

'Yes,' Micawber said. 'I am confident that advantages will be as abundant as the fish in the sea, and the availability of numerous occupations will not be sparse, so I will no longer have to rely on serendipitous employment. In short, something is bound to turn up!'